I0764546

Except for select brand names, locations and businesses, this book is a work of fiction. Names, places, events and characters are fictitious. Any similarities to actual events or persons, living or dead, are purely coincidental.

Cougar Tales

ISBN 978-1-934446-98-0

Cover Design by *Viper*

Published by

Romance Divine LLC

www.romancedivine.com

Cougar Tales

J.A. Rawls

Dedicated with love to my family, who make the twists and turns in each of my stories more in tune with life's drama.

Cougar Awakening

Women with "pasts" interest men because men hope that history will repeat itself.
Mae West

Cougar: "A large, powerful, tawny brown cat, formerly widespread in the Americas, but now extinct in many areas."
(Webster's Seventh Collegiate Dictionary, 1971)

One

Jana didn't know if she was happy or not, never gave it much thought anymore. She'd moved on after Craig, and now there was work, the company, HER company. She was successful, at work, in business; but her personal life? As a woman...?

*****

Jana sorted through the folders on her desk, trying to bring order out of chaos, when Charlie walked into her office. He smiled, that shy, awkward smile which meant he had something on his mind and was debating whether to tell her or not. Jana returned his smile reluctantly, "Yes, can I help you?"

"Boss, did you realize that people were intimidated by your comments in today's meeting?"

"You mean the meeting with the idiot accountants?"

"Yes, that one."

"Of course I knew; that was my intent! They come to meetings and bring me nothing but problems; but they never offer any solutions. They want me to tell them what to do. I pay them a lot of money to take care of this, but they can't seem to handle even a simple task. It gets old, believe me, very old."

"But boss, did you see their faces?"

"Of course, Charlie, I saw their faces," Jana huffed. "Unfortunately all I ever see is that 'deer-in-the-headlight' look!"

"Well, yea, some of that was going on," Charlie shrugged. "But most of those guys were lusting after you, drooling over every syllable you uttered. They're in awe of you." He paused; now was the time to get to the point. "You're their cougar!"

"We do not lust and drool in meetings Charlie—I'm their what?" Jana leaned back in her chair, her eyes locked on her faithful, and surprising, assistant.

"A cougar, they're drawn to you."

"Very funny Charlie, cougar indeed, go home and let me get some work done. Right now I don't want to be anyone's kitten, or even their cat for that matter." Jana snarled, brandishing her manicured ruby red nails as mock claws.

Charlie laughed as he backed out of the room. *She doesn't get it,* he thought. He knew men in the office, especially the younger ones, were attracted to her. Hell it wasn't just the young ones, but they were the most obvious about it. He visualized the 'cougar in her den' on the way to his office. *Boss you're a cougar, you just don't realize it.*

As he walked out of the building, he noticed Jana's car, that silver BMW. *Yes, she's a cougar, a cougar in denial. I need to tell her more about what she does to the men around her. I know she doesn't realize what real power she has.* Charlie squeezed into his Mini Cooper and laughed to himself. *She's great to work for, but she's naïve. She has so much untapped power. One of my jobs, one I'll assign to myself, will be to unleash that power.*

Jana looked out her window and watched Charlie drive out of the parking garage. She smiled to herself thinking about what he'd said, and trying to figure out what he'd meant. *No time now, I'll have to talk to him more about this tomorrow.*

She returned to sorting through the papers on her desk, trying to get herself organized. Jana hated leaving the office at the end of the day without knowing exactly what to expect when she returned the next morning. It was this attention to detail that allowed her to rise to owner and CEO. On her 'To Do' list she made a note to have Charlie set up a meeting with Mike in Accounting. Thinking about it made her cringe. *I'll fix this accounting problem. The additional costs I've paid due to their negligence will stop. Tomorrow, I'll put an end to this foolishness once and for all or know the reason why, yes, tomorrow!*

Jana leaned back in her chair, surveying her surroundings. Her office space, featured in a recent *Architectural Digest* article on women making their mark in big business, fully expressed the beauty and functionality of the space. The building design, and in particular her office, allowed her to sit at her desk and watch the sun rise and set simply by turning her chair left or right. It was the primary reason she'd hired the young, good looking architect. He was the only one who understood the importance of her office tranquility. After all when you spend sixty plus hours a week in your office, other than a private bathroom, ambiance was everything.

What did Charlie mean by cougar? I've been called a lot of things on my way up the corporate ladder, but a cougar? Never. Jana reached over and pulled her old standby Webster's II, soft cover, dictionary from the shelf by her computer.

She flipped through the pages to look up the word 'cougar'. She wanted to see if there was a definition listed that she wasn't familiar with. The dictionary defined a cougar as a mountain lion, *okay not a great dictionary.* Jana slid over to her computer and did a search on cougar. What she found startled her. It said a cougar is a large, solitary cat…*Was Charlie referring to my size? No, he wouldn't do that.* A cougar is the second heaviest cat…*There's that weight thing again, but I can't believe that's his intent.* The definition further said that a cougar was secretive and avoided people. *That fits me to a "T". Cougar…what did Charlie mean? Oh hell, it's time to go home.*

*****

Jana entered her condo, flipped on the lights and dead-bolted the door. She was tired, but a good tired, if that was possible. Entering the kitchen she smiled at the clicking sound her heels made on the marble tiles. *Craig used to love that sound...Jana, stop it!*

Dining on a simple chicken Caesar salad and iced tea in her favorite crystal wine glass, she lit a candle and enjoyed a quiet supper. As she ate, her thoughts returned to Charlie's comments about the Cougar. *What was he trying to tell me? What did he mean? I'll have to get to the bottom of all this, but not tonight. I need relaxation and a good night's sleep.*

She turned down the bed, ruminating on the significance of this simple ritual act. *Craig would have done that, in fact he always did it, but that's in the past and this is now.* She still missed his companionship. At one time he had been her husband, lover best friend and then, for some reason, everything fell apart. As she gazed around the room she thought more about her failed marriage. She and Craig had shared everything, their hopes, their dreams, and now sadly a divorce. They were both to blame for the split. They grew apart and when things finally came to a head, they had agreed it was best to go their separate ways. The nights were always their special time, or at least they had been. *Enough, enough! This is not the time to feel sorry for yourself!* She put the day's events out of her mind and fell into a deep sleep.

The alarm was incessant. Jana reached over and turned it off. Her mind started working the minute her eyes were open. Another day, another dollar or two, she smiled. A hot shower was definitely in order.

*****

Dressed in a black Armani suit with a lime green shell, Jana slid behind the wheel of her BMW, coffee in hand. She engaged her hands-free cell to call the office and get things in motion before she arrived. "Charlie, is that you?"

"Who did you expect?"

"Don't get funny. Are you in the office?"

"Isn't that the number you called?"

"Cute." *He's not making this easy, guess he hasn't had his coffee yet.* "Charlie, set up a meeting with Mike from Accounting for seven-thirty. And, Charlie, don't be so grouchy when I get there. Whatever the problem is, fix it now." She cut off the call and smiled. *That would keep him talking to himself for a few minutes*.

*****

Jana entered the office and stopped at Charlie's door. "Did you get my meeting set up with Mike?"

"Of course, isn't that what you wanted me to do?"

"Charlie, did your mother ever tell you not to answer a question with a question?"

"No, why?"

"Charlie, give me a break, please. I need to talk to you if you have a couple of minutes. Now would be good."

"Sure, not a problem, do I need to bring anything?"

"No, I just have a couple of questions from our discussion yesterday."

Charlie smiled. He knew exactly what she wanted to talk about and he was not going to make it easy for her.

Jana dropped her purse in her desk drawer, "So, Charlie, how was your evening?"

"It was fine, how about yours?"

"I have to admit some of your comments yesterday would not let me rest, that 'cougar' thing for example. What exactly does cougar mean, based on your definition?"

"Boss, you're out of touch. You really don't know, do you?"

"Charlie, you're beginning to frustrate me, and I know you realize that. Believe me if I knew what you meant by the comment I wouldn't be asking you now. So give, what exactly does it mean in Charlie speak?"

"Boss, it isn't Charlie speak, it everyone's definition, except yours. You don't have anything in your hands do you?"

Jana raised her hands so he could see they were empty. "Charlie, what gives?"

"Okay! A cougar is a female who is older, sophisticated, beautiful, and who attracts younger men. That's the definition of a 'cougar'."

Jana closed her eyes, shook her head and then looked up. "You *really* don't believe I fit that definition, do you?"

"Yes, boss, that's you! Remember the meeting yesterday?"

"Of course I remember the meeting yesterday. It was one of the worst meetings I've had with our accountants."

"Well," Charlie shrugged, "there is that. But think about the way they looked at you when you spoke to them."

"Yes, I remember. There was not one of them without that 'deer in the headlight' look. I couldn't believe how stupid they appeared. Hell, they couldn't even put a full sentence together without stumbling over the words. I actually had a problem following their thought processes, assuming they had any."

"No boss, beyond the stammering. Those guys are all MBA graduates with CPA credentials. They're all extremely intelligent, they know their jobs, but they have trouble communicating with you."

"You could have fooled me. If the meeting yesterday was the best they have, I need new accountants."

Charlie sighed, *she's gonna be a tough sell.* "Boss those guys are enamored by you. They are flat, tongues out, drooling over you as a woman, a woman of power."

Jana's mouth hit the floor. She couldn't believe what she was being told. "Charlie what kind of drugs are you on?"

"No drugs, honest, boss you *are* beautiful. You're powerful, and those guys recognize it and want to follow you around like puppies."

"Charlie, I don't have pets for a reason and I don't want my accountants following me around like puppies." Jana slumped into her chair, thoughts of a Hurricane her only salvation. *Isn't it five o'clock somewhere?* "Charlie, I'm having trouble grasping all of this. You need to get back to work and I need to see Mike. You really need to re-think your 'cougar' theory and its applicability to me. I truly believe you're way off base."

"Boss, I'll think about it, but I'm telling you I'm right on the mark. These guys want to be more than employees. Try it out at the cocktail party this afternoon and see. If you give even one of them the go ahead, he'll fall all over himself to make anything you want happen."

"Okay Charlie, I'll consider it, but I think you're nuts. I've a meeting to prepare for. Get Mike from accounting." Jana pulled two files from her briefcase, and then gave Charlie a puzzled look. "How old would you say Mike is?"

"Age, I would say early thirties, why?"

"Just thinking about what you said." Jana smiled as she leaned back in her chair. "Take that stupid smirk off your face and get Mike in here."

Charlie walked out of her office without saying another word. He was smiling from ear to ear as Mike approached from the elevator. *Jana was really thinking about being a 'cougar'. Excellent! Maybe I should warn Mike, then again maybe not. He's a big boy...or so time will tell.*

Jana's thoughts were going a mile a minute. *Charlie is nuts. This can't be how people see me, how young men see me, it just can't. I'm old enough to be their mother for heaven's sake.*

Enough, enough, I need to get to work. Charlie's mention of the social function reminded her she had invited several key clients to the office for cocktails and she was joining them for dinner. Many of her staff were invited, even some of the accountants. The good news is that she always kept a black dress in her office and could get party-ready without having to make a trip home.

Before she turned on her computer there was a soft knock on her door. *Crap it's got to be Mike.* "Door's open."

Mike formally entered the office as if he was reporting to a military superior. "Good morning ma'am."

Jana bristled at the '*ma'am'.* "Good morning, Mike. I'll make this quick as I've another meeting to prepare for. I need your staff to work up the numbers for the expense accounts of my ten top executives. I need these identified by type of costs and summarized by individual, purpose, and division for the past six months. Can you have it ready to brief my staff by noon tomorrow?"

"Yes, ma'am, that shouldn't be a problem."

If he calls me ma'am one more time I'm going to throw up. "Okay, good. Please provide the info to Charlie. I'll need individual packets tomorrow for the meeting which is currently scheduled for noon. I'd like you at the meeting to field any questions. Provide me a draft copy by this afternoon before I leave the office so I can review it and make any changes before the meeting. I'm interested in any anomalies you discover; any questions?"

"No questions; I'll take care of it personally. Will there be anything else?"

"No, that'll be all." Jana sat back in her chair and crossed her legs. She caught Mike's eyes with her own and smiled. "Mike, are you planning to attend the cocktail party this afternoon?"

"Yes, ma'am, I'll be there, see you then." Mike blushed and backed out of the office.

Jana didn't know what to think. She hadn't even touched

him and he left her office blushing. All she'd done was ask him if he was going to the cocktail party. She flipped through her schedule and wondered about the 'cougar' comment Charlie made. "Damn you Charlie!" Jana left her office and went to the conference room. As she walked in the room, the young man behind the podium looked as if he was about to wet himself. *Charlie, it isn't ardor these young men are feeling, it's fear,* she smiled as she took her seat.

Two

A drink was in order. Jana's day was busy with one meeting after another. She had a cocktail party to host in less than thirty minutes and she still needed to change clothes. Walking to the bathroom she noticed Charlie had already put out her dress, *he thinks of everything. What would I do without him?* She studied the image in the mirror and had to admit, the face that looked back at her 'was' attractive. She'd aged well. Her shoulder length dishwater blonde hair framed an oval face, but it was her dazzling green eyes that drew the attention. *Maybe Charlie is right.* She took the dress off the hanger and slipped it over her head. With her hands on her hips she put a sexy pout on her face and then laughed at herself. *A 'cougar' indeed.*

Jana knew she needed to hurry, or she was going to be more than fashionably late. She touched up her makeup. A pair of chandelier earrings accented her long neck and drew attention to the open cowl neckline of her dress. It was a beautiful dress, sleek and clingy but with enough body to give it a life of its own.

Jana hadn't taken time to reflect on Charlie's comments, nor had she thought about Mike's reactions to her this morning. From the bathroom she heard Charlie's voice over the intercom advising her that her guests were beginning to arrive. Running her fingers through her hair, she stepped back and took one last look.

I look fantastic if I have to say so myself, she smiled. She exchanged her business pumps for a sexy pair of stilettos. *I'm ready. Let's do it.*

A hush fell over the small crowd as Jana walked into the room. Charlie approached, taking her hand in his arm and escorting her to the bar. "What can I get you to drink, boss?"

"Just a diet 7-Up if they have it." She smiled as she scanned the room.

"Boss, they always have diet 7-Up, as the caterer knows they would be fired if they didn't have your favorite drink." Charlie ordered a tall diet 7-Up and a beer.

Jana smiled as she accepted the drink. "So, Charlie, how is everything going? Have the folks been here long? Is there anyone I need to single out to spend some time with? Any issues I need to be aware of before I get started?"

"Boss, which question would you like me to answer first?"

"All of them, Charlie, in the exact order I asked them!"

"Okay here goes. Things are going well. Everyone is ahead of you in the drinking department, but that's not unusual. They've all been here for at least ten minutes, but some have been here as long as twenty. No, there is no one in particular you need to spend time with. This is strictly a social event, a chance for your staff to put some faces with names for our key clients. There are no issues so just have fun and enjoy yourself." Charlie lifted his glass and downed half of his beer. "Don't forget you're a *cougar*; you need to try that role."

"Charlie, I repeat, you're crazy, but thanks for the info. I do intend to enjoy myself and I will take into consideration your *cougar* comment. Understand I'm no one's cat." She smiled as she went to her guests. She worked the room for thirty minutes: greeting, smiling, glad-handing, asking about children and spouses. *Such power such control, I love it; it's exhilarating and exhausting at the same time.*

She noticed Mike waiting in line at the bar, and took a

moment to consider him. He wasn't bad looking; in fact he was quite handsome. *I bet he wouldn't be happy if I told him he reminded me of a little boy all dressed up in his suit for Church.* Jana smiled and watched him. He seemed to be gazing at her with a desperate look on his face. *He is attractive...let's try this cougar stuff on for size.*

Accentuating each movement for his benefit, she floated towards him and watched the color drain from his face. "Mike, are you okay?"

"Yes, ma'am very fine. I've been watching you work your magic."

"Magic? You mean watching me do my job don't you?"

"Yes, ma'am, but you do it so easily and without a care in the world. It doesn't really look like work to me—at least not the way you do it."

Jana couldn't believe her eyes and ears. This young man, maybe in his early thirties was flirting with her. She decided to keep talking or he was going to slobber all over himself. "So, Mike, how do you like working for me?"

"Oh, ma'am, I like it a lot. You're the best, even when you're angry with what we do; it's great to work for you."

Jana leaned forward and softly whispered, "Mike, quit calling me ma'am."

"Yes ma'am, sorry ma'am," Mike bit down on his lower lip realizing he'd not only said ma'am once but twice.

"Mike, would you do me a favor?"

"Absolutely, anything, just ask!" He was blushing again.

"When you get your drink will you order me a diet 7-Up?"

"Yes ma'am, uh, Ms Jana, I'll take care of that right now." Mike turned and immediately ran into the person in front of him. The line to the bar had not moved at all.

Jana patted his arm. "Mike I'm going to sit down over there by that big palm plant. Please join me when you have the drinks."

"Not a problem, I'll be there as soon as I can."

Mike watched her walk away, stopping to talk to two executives; her movements were exquisite as she established a position of authority on the sofa. She looked like a queen holding court, a queen with her legs crossed and her four-inch stiletto rocking back and forth. He smiled; this was the end to a perfect day, a day starting with a meeting in Jana's office.

Jana couldn't believe it. Mike had to be pulling her leg. He behaved like one of those little boys on the school grounds that had a chance to hold hands with his best girl. Surely that wasn't what was going on here.

Charlie approached her with a grin on his face. "Told you so," he chuckled and walked off.

Mike returned, looking pleased. He had two diet 7-Ups, one in each hand. Jana looked at him with a questioning stare.

Mike smiled, "I figured if you really like these I should learn to like them too."

Jana rolled her eyes and took a long drink. *Where is a gun when you need it? Okay, let me try something else here.* "Mike, were you planning on attending the dinner tonight?"

"I thought about it, but I hadn't made up my mind for sure, why?"

Jana sipped at her drink, her green eyes peering over the top of the glass. "Would you mind being my escort for the evening?" She smiled a seductive smile—at least she hoped it was seductive. It had been a l-o-n-g time since she'd been consciously seductive.

"Oh, ma'am, that would be fantastic!"

She gently touched his arm. "Mike, you can't do it if you call me ma'am anymore. Call me Jana; call me Ms Jana, but not ma'am, please."

"Yes, Ms Jana, I can do that and I'd love to be your escort this evening. I'll even drive if you like. I can bring you back here if you want, or I can see if I can get one of the staff to take your car to your house. Then I can drop you off there after dinner."

Jana fought to suppress a chuckle. Her young paramour was obviously excited. "Don't worry Mike; I'll have Charlie take care of my car. It would be nice to be driven for a change. I would also be honored if you escorted me home."

Mike blushed from head to toe. He knew he was doing it, but every time he thought about how lucky he was to be escorting Ms Jana to dinner he blushed again. He found Charlie and informed him that Jana requested he take her car home. "Charlie, she asked me to escort her to dinner tonight."

Charlie smiled. *Perhaps Jana would make this work. Maybe, just maybe she would let this young man show her the woman she was, and could be.* He whispered to Mike, "Hold on tight brother, you are headed for one hell of a ride."

Mike recoiled in shock, then grinned and walked away. He scanned the room to find Jana. It was time to leave for dinner and he wanted to make sure she was ready. His heart fell when he found her talking to an older gentleman, slender, about her height. Jana was laughing and leaned over to kiss the man on the lips. Mike walked up and stood next to her.

Jana acknowledged him with a nod and a wink. "Craig, this is Mike, my escort for the evening. Mike, this is Craig, my ex-husband," she looked from one to the other waiting for a reaction.

"Nice to meet you, Mike," Craig gave Jana a questioning look.

"Nice meeting you, Sir," Mike responded as he stepped alongside Jana reaching for her hand and placing it at the bend of his arm.

Jana watched Craig's eyebrow rise slightly. "We better be off, don't want to be late. It was good to see you Craig, talk to you later."

They walked to Mike's BMW SUV. Jana was impressed; this was a young man with taste. *Who knew? Maybe this evening wouldn't be a total loss. If I could only get him to talk in full sentences it would be better.* Mike opened the door and helped her in. It was quite a step up for a woman in high heels and a slim black cocktail dress, but she managed elegantly.

"Do you mind stopping," Jana pointed to the corner ahead, "at the little store up on our right so I can pick up some cigarettes?"

"Not a problem. What brand do you smoke? I'll get them for you." He couldn't remember her ever smoking. But if she wanted cigarettes he would get them for her.

"A package of the vanilla flavored cigarillos. The smaller ones please, as they fit nicely in my cigarette case. I don't smoke that much, but it's often nice to enjoy one when I drink." She took money from her purse and handed it to him.

He returned with the cigarillos.

"I appreciate you stopping and getting these for me. I meant to get them at lunch today, but I never got out of the office." She opened the package, removed one and handed Mike the matches.

Lighting the cigarillo, Mike inquired, "You never had lunch?"

"No, unfortunately that happens a lot. I usually eat lunch in the early afternoon, but that depends on my schedule."

"Why doesn't Charlie block time on your calendar for lunch every day?"

"You know we tried that once, but I still didn't eat when I should have, and blocking out time on my calendar just made my days longer. What kind of hours do you work as one of our contractors?" She lowered her window so that her smoke didn't fill the car.

"Actually I usually work mornings here and afternoons at the corporate office. I try to get to work early. I can get a lot done before the rest of my staff shows up." He watched her finish the cigarillo, imagining what her luscious lips could do to him. *How can she be so casual and relaxed, can't she feel the energy between us?*

"Yes, I know the feeling. Those first few hours in the morning are probably my most productive." She reached over and patted Mike on the arm, a friendly gesture on her part, but one that sent Mike's senses reeling.

She touched me. This is the best day of my life. Mike continued to drive with a Cheshire cat grin on his face.

Jana couldn't figure out what made him smile, and she found it hard to believe it was because she had touched his sleeve. She hadn't even touched skin! She was going to test Charlie's theory when she arrived at the restaurant. *Let's see how he handles this next one if a simple touch is what put that look on his face.*

When Mike parked the SUV and came around to help Jana out she virtually slid off the seat. Reaching forward he collected her into his arms, his face falling into her hair, catching her scent. For a moment he held her close, reveling in the heat and softness that his arms enfolded. She kissed him on the cheek. "Thanks Mike, you saved me a broken ankle. Sometimes I forget that I have these heels on."

She turned and strutted away, pausing to turn again and look him in the eye, "Are you coming?"

He was trying to understand what just happened. *Did she kiss me? Yes, and it was great.* His eyes focused on her legs and the stilettos she wore. *I love those shoes, but maybe they aren't a good idea. What am I saying, they're a great idea. They make her legs sexy and show off the most beautiful calves I've ever seen. This evening just gets better and better.*

Mike and Jana entered the restaurant, aware of the quizzical looks they gathered. Jana stifled a chuckle; *they're probably trying to figure out if I'm with my son.* Jana leaned close to Mike and whispered in his ear, "Let me lead the way."

Mike acknowledged her with a nod of his head, maneuvered her in front of him at the same time placing his hands possessively at her waist, and stepping behind her as they moved through the throng of people.

Jana smiled and led Mike through the crowd. *That should set the tongues wagging.*

Entering the banquet room, Jana walked to the head table. Mike stopped her, questioning her with his eyes on whether he should follow or find another seat. She took his hand and led him to their seats. Mike was with Jana, in front of his peers, and no one seemed to question that. Some of his friends were smiling and giving him a thumb's up. *What are they thinking? Who cares, I'm with Jana. The night just gets better and better.*

Mike struggled to remember his Grandmother's admonitions about 'what a gentleman does', he held out Jana's chair seating her at the table, and mimicked her as she unfolded the linen napkin and laid it on her lap. He was going to have to watch her close because his idea of a night out was pizza and beer. Hell, there was more silverware by his plate than he had in his entire kitchen. *This could be fun, if I don't screw it up.*

When salads miraculously appeared, Jana took the smallest fork to the left of her plate and Mike followed her lead. *This woman is so elegant, so sophisticated and tonight she's with me.*

Jana knew he was watching her and mimicking everything she did. *I ought to eat the salad with my desert spoon and see what he does.* She smiled at Mike and began eating. As she crossed her legs, her napkin slipped to the floor between them. Both she and Mike reached for it and they bumped heads.

Mike retrieved her napkin and handed it to her, "Sorry."

"Not a problem, no damage done." She laid her right hand over his, gave it a squeeze, and watched Mike blush as if she had ripped off his clothes. *Oh no, where did that thought come from!* She needed to concentrate on getting through the meal without embarrassing either of them.

Mike surveyed the crowd and noticed several of his

colleagues watching him. He smiled and acknowledged their eye contact. He could only surmise what they were talking about. He wasn't worried about his current circumstances; after all sitting at the head table with the boss wasn't all that unusual. Well, perhaps it was for him, but as the lead CPA for the firm he didn't see it as a problem. Actually he was still trying to figure out exactly how he'd gotten so lucky.

Jana whispered, "Penny for your thoughts." She touched his arm.

"You'd be getting the short end of that deal, I'm afraid." Mike covered her hand with his.

"Do you mind if I ask you a couple of personal questions?"

"No, not at all."

"Okay, how long have you worked for me?"

"Let's see, I've been a CPA for about six years. I came to work for this company two years ago, about the same time you contracted with us for accounting support."

"That's right," Jana paused, "you don't exactly work for me."

"True, as an independent contractor I work *with* you and not *for* you." Mike studied Jana, trying to figure out where her semantic line of investigation was heading. "There *is* a fine line between the two."

"There is definitely a difference. That said," Jana's eyes met Mike's, "do you have trouble remembering where your loyalties lay?"

"No, at least not normally. I know my staff and I work with you, but I also know I work for you as you, your company, ultimately pay the bills for our services. If I don't provide you the services you are expecting then our business relationship suffers."

Jana nodded and they continued to discuss business over dessert and coffee. She watched a small trio setting up; they would have dancing after the meal. She thought that was wonderful as she loved to dance. "Mike, do you dance?"

"Yes, I do after a fashion. My mom made me take lessons when I was younger. It's been a while, but I'm sure I can hold my own."

The band began with a soft ballad that had Jana humming the melody. Mike leaned over and took her hand, drawing her eyes to his as he stood. "May I have this dance?"

"Thank you Mike, I would love to dance with you." A sexy Rumba was just what she needed. Smiling, they took the floor. Although they were not the only couple dancing, they appeared to be the only couple who knew what they were doing.

Mike watched the crowd as he danced with Jana. He particularly noticed her ex-husband watching them intently. Mike knew she'd been divorced for some time, but the man appeared to be in pain.

Jana closed her eyes and swayed to the soft rhythm of the music. Her feet hurt and she knew dancing in the stilettos was going to give her nightmares, but she didn't care. She was enjoying herself beyond measure. It'd been years, literally years, since a man had held her in their arms and danced with her, danced with her like he wanted to hold her forever. Mike was good for her ego, but what could she do for him? The music ended too soon, and Mike escorted her back to the table, his arm firmly around her waist.

Jana watched him for a few minutes and decided they needed to leave. She wanted to take this to the next level, and she couldn't do it here with everyone watching. "Let's call it an evening, okay."

"Absolutely, do you need to say your good-byes, or can we just leave?"

"No, let's just leave. Charlie will handle it from here." She caught Charlie's attention as she picked up her purse to leave. He smiled and mouthed the word *C-O-U-G-A-R* to her. She winked as she walked by his table and patted him on the shoulder. "Don't wait up for me."

Charlie laughed out loud and Mike looked back at him with a quizzical look. “What was that all about?”

Jana gave Mike a slow and sensuous smile. “Believe it or not, it was about a cat. Don’t ask!”

Three

Jana relaxed in the SUV allowing Mike to light another cigarillo for her. It'd been longer than she could remember when she'd spent a more enjoyable evening. As they approached her condo, Jana wondered whether she should invite Mike in for a drink or not. Glancing over at him, she smiled. He was quite handsome: sandy brown hair cut in a military style, large brown eyes and a smile that was to die for. No, it was too early for this night to be over; she definitely wanted Mike to stay longer.

It didn't hurt that Mike didn't work directly for her. In fact, it made being with him a lot easier for her to rationalize. When she and Craig got their divorce, several of the single men in her company asked her out. She quickly realized it was hard to kiss someone one day, and admonish them the next for not doing their jobs. As a contractor for her company he worked with her, but not for her-exactly. *Maybe I can expand our 'working together' premise. Yes, that is exactly what I want to do, the question is how.*

Mike parked the car, "Your chariot has arrived."

Jana shifted slightly facing him, "Would the chariot driver like to come in for a night cap?"

"Actually, your chariot driver would enjoy that very much." He blushed. *I wonder what she expects me to do. I'll just follow her lead.*

Jana took her keys from her purse and handed them to him so he could be chivalrous and unlock the door. He'd been a perfect gentleman all night, time now to figure out what else he was good for.

Mike stumbled for the right words. "I had a great time tonight, and I want to thank you for letting me be your escort for the evening."

Jana turned, stepped up to him and lightly kissed him on the lips. "I had a wonderful time too. Please come in and I'll get us a drink."

He put his hands on her shoulders and gently pulled her back to face him. He was now the aggressor, moving in to deepen the second kiss. Mike couldn't move fast enough to get her as close to him as was physically possible.

His erection pushed against her hips, and there was no doubt in Jana's mind that he was attracted to her. As much as she wanted to continue, the foyer of her condo was *not* the place to let that happen. She took Mike's hand and pulled him into the condo, quickly closing the door. "We can continue this here if you like, but I think we would both be more comfortable in the living room. What will it be a night cap, or would you prefer coffee?"

"I think a night cap." Mike replied as he took a seat on her cream-colored, leather sofa. He tried to relax as he waited for his drink, but he couldn't control his thoughts; they seemed to be rampant. Jana poured them both a clear drink from a decorative decanter. He was hesitant to ask her what it was since he didn't like hard liquor, but he wanted to appear sophisticated. Mike casually took the glass as he watched Jana down her drink in one swallow. Following her lead he nonchalantly did the same, and thought his ears were going to start on fire. Gagging and stuttering he asked, "What—what was that stuff?"

"Grappa."

Beads of perspiration broke out on his forehead, "What's Grappa?"

"It's Italian, the pressings from the seeds and stems of the grapes after the harvest, it's a digestive. I'm truly sorry; I forget how strong a drink it is if you've never had it before. I grew accustomed to it while I was in Europe, and while it's strong it does settle the stomach. I'll admit it's an acquired taste. Didn't you like it?"

"It was a surprise is all." He smiled shyly; the woman was full of surprises.

"Can I get you something else?"

He wiped his mouth with his hands, "No, I'm fine, thanks."

"Mike, I hate to talk about work, but did you happen to finish those expense account breakdowns for me?"

"Sure, I gave a copy as you requested to Charlie before I left the office today. Did you get a chance to look at it?"

"Unfortunately no, and I left the office without them. Damn, I wanted to look it over before the meeting in the morning. Oh well." She frowned and poured herself another drink.

"It isn't a problem I have a copy in the car. If you want I'll go get it and we can go over it now."

"That would be wonderful, if you don't have some place you need to be. I'd hate to hold you up if you have other plans."

"No other plans, I'm yours for the evening. Give me a minute while I get my briefcase."

Mine for the evening, now that's something I can sink my teeth into. I wonder what it would take to get him to spend the night. Maybe we could discuss his report in my bed. My God! Two kisses and I already have him naked in my bed?

She needed to get her thoughts back on the job and not on assaulting Mike's gorgeous body. She lit another cigarillo and enjoyed the slight buzz the stimulant provided.

Mike entered the room, and watched Jana smoke. The aroma of the vanilla scented cigarillo permeated the air, as soft smoke rose around her. The lit end seemed to glow like a fire started more from the woman who held it than a match. Just watching her enjoy this simple pleasure excited him. She was beautiful, and the power that exuded from her was something he could almost touch. He struggled to focus, "Do you want to go over this now?"

"Yes, I had a reason for asking for these, which I'm sure you've already guessed, but let me explain. You know Daryl and Mark just returned from a trip to Macau, right?"

"Sure, I saw their expense reports and my staff reviewed them, but we haven't paid them yet. In fact when I was going through this for you today there were some charges that seemed, well, let me say they didn't appear appropriate."

"Mike before we get any further into the details on this would you please pour me another Grappa. Get one for yourself as well if you like."

"I'll be glad to get you a refill, but I'll pass thanks." He handed her the drink and watched Jana again down the drink in one swallow. *This is one hell of a woman I'm spending time with.*

"Okay, I'm ready now, what did you notice?"

"Daryl had several charges for meals that exceeded the maximum amount we pay for daily costs. In fact his costs appeared, at least to me, to be excessive for the entire trip. If he ate that much in food each day he would've put on ten to fifteen pounds without a problem. It seems to me he padded his expense account to get the maximum allowed."

Jana sighed with the realization that her suspicions were valid. "Would your staff have caught this through their normal review of the expense records?"

"No, it would've never been questioned because it didn't exceed what was allowed. But I looked at a similar trip last month for two of my people, and the costs were less than half. If they were the ones to review the reports, they would have questioned the costs, so, yea maybe."

"What about Mark's?"

"His were the same, excessive, but different. In Mark's

case he inflated his lodging costs. I know the hotel they stayed in was $163 per night and that is exactly what Daryl claimed. But Mark claimed his costs were $361. I thought at first it was just a simple mistake, a transposition error, but the actual receipts were different. I'm guessing they were changed since they didn't match Daryl's, and I know they stayed at the same place."

Jana wrung her hands as she listened to Mike's comments. "I was hoping this wasn't the case, even though I was pretty sure it was. Last week I did some comparison of travel costs and expense records for different divisions and I found some glaring differences when they had all made this trip together. It was too big a difference when you laid it all out side by side. That's the reason I asked you to take a look at the records of all my managers. I didn't want to single anyone out, but I figured if you uncovered it in a review of all the accounts then I could take appropriate action. I have a meeting scheduled tomorrow morning at ten and I want you there."

Mike was quiet, trying to put everything together. "Yes, I'll be there. You truly aren't surprised by this?" *Had this evening simply been about uncovering fraud at work, or is she really interested in me?*

"No," Jana stared across the room, "not surprised, but very disappointed."

"What do you want me to do?"

"Actually nothing with this, I'll take it from here. My intent is to give them a chance to fall on their sword and come clean, but it doesn't matter whether they do or not, as the end state will be the same."

"I'm sorry Jana. Do you need me to act as a witness?"

"No, not a witness, you're my accountant and you'll provide nothing but the facts. I'll take care of everything else."

Mike watched her face. Her emotions were all over the place, he could see it as her eyes moved and her mouth tensed. He never wanted to be on the bad side of this woman. *I actually feel sorry for Daryl and Mark, but stupid is the only way to describe what they did, losing their jobs for chump change.* "I'm glad I could help, I think?"

Jana leaned toward him placing her hand on his crotch. "I know this is hard," the double-entendre lost on neither of them, "but I really need you—now."

Mike's physical response was immediate. His penis ached for her touch and its freedom. He pulled her into his arms and she melted into him.

Jana lifted her head and looked into Mike's eyes. She smiled at the thought of the things he could do to make everything better. "Stay with me tonight."

He was momentarily tongue tied, not knowing exactly how to address her request. "Jana, this isn't a good idea. I know you're troubled by this work thing, but sex isn't the answer."

"It's not just sex, I want you to make love to me, and *yes*, it is the answer." Her finger lightly traced a line around his lips, "Let me assure you I don't normally bring young men home and molest them."

He brushed a stray bit of hair from her eyes and smiled, "I never thought you did. But Jana there could be fallout from your staff if we take this step."

"What fall out? We're consenting adults; we both know what we need and what we want."

"Yes, I'm sure of that, but this could get...complicated."

She pushed herself away from him to look him in the eyes. "Why?"

"I know my company hasn't notified you yet, but I tendered my resignation yesterday. I've been offered a partnership with my uncle in Las Vegas. I'll be the CEO; it's something I've been wanting since I started. I finally have enough saved to make it happen. I gave my notice and will leave in two weeks. As much as I would love to be with you, to make love to you and to stay with you now, I'm not into one night stands."

"It doesn't have to be a one night stand," she laughed. "It can be two, three, four, eight, however many days until you leave."

"Jana, that isn't funny."

"Can't we just take this a day at a time? I don't want you to change your plans, but I would like to know you just a little better."

"I don't know." Mike's mind raced through all the possibilities, advantages and liabilities of a liaison with this formidable woman. "I'm not sure I'll be able to walk away if we get involved. I don't want to hurt you."

"We're adults Mike. I know what I'm doing. But even adults need to be loved. I don't want to marry you," her lips formed a sexy pout, "I just want to use and abuse you."

Mike tried to relax, unsure exactly how to respond. "Yes—I'd love to spend the night, and as many other nights as we can work into our schedules before I leave. But Jana, I *am* leaving." He leaned down and tasted her lips, slowing kissing her while running his tongue across her closed mouth.

Jana gently opened her mouth for the assault. The kiss ended and she lost herself in Mike's eyes. "I understand, and I'm okay with that." She slipped her arms around his neck and Mike lifted her to straddle his lap. They effortlessly moved into each other, Mike massaging her back with one hand while the other explored her body. He softly eased his hand under the hem of her dress, felt a bump, and looked at her in shock.

"My garter belt, is that a problem?"

"Not a problem for me. I don't think I've ever been with a woman who wore a garter belt. I've thought about it a few times, fantasized about it a thousand times, but never imagined it could really happen. Most of the women I know wear panty hose. I just assumed you did too."

She narrowed her eyes and snapped a garter strap with one of her manicured nails. "Wearing a garter belt makes me feel sexy.

A lot of women buy things to satisfy their boyfriends or husbands. I buy it for me. I love satin and lace, and if I feel sexy then the man I am with will feel that way about me as well. Do you agree?"

"Where is your bedroom?"

Jana stood and took Mike's hand. "Let me show you. It's one of my favorite rooms and I know you'll love it."

As they walked hand-in-hand down the hall, Mike couldn't stop smiling. He was in Jana's condo and she was leading him to her bedroom. He just hoped he wasn't dreaming.

Four

Jana released his hand and turned on the lights as they entered the bedroom. The room was beautiful and handsome at the same time. Mike took it all in. It wasn't a frilly room, but was one you knew a woman lived in: exquisite figurines on the tables, pillows arrayed on the bed; and a beautiful throw across the settee. The colors were tranquil, turquoise on a single wall accenting the rest of the room in soft beiges, mauves and browns. It was elegant, tasteful yet homey and relaxing. "It's a nice room, very inviting."

She wanted him to like it, and he didn't disappoint her. "When I got my divorce, this was the only place I felt comfortable. I'd come home from the office, pour myself a drink, and come in here to relax. I'm pleased you like it."

Mike ran his hands along her hips and down her thighs. He lifted her black dress over her head and laid it on the chair. He gazed at this beautiful woman standing majestic in her high heels, garter belt and stockings, lace panties and matching demi-cup bra. The rush of blood to his penis was painful and he grimaced as he felt his erection grow harder.

Jana licked her lips, enjoying his reaction and manly attributes. She knew by his physical reaction that he was pleased with what stood before him. He already had her dress off, and that was further than any other man had gotten since Craig.

Mike moved closer, taking her in his arms. His hands

couldn't stay still. They seemed to be everywhere, taking her to that special place and he was going to make sure she enjoyed the trip. "I think I've got too many clothes on compared to you." He removed his jacket and tie, never taking his eyes off her. They leaned into each other for another kiss. She parted her lips as their tongues met. "So what now boss lady?"

"You mean you don't know what to do now?" Jana grinned and thought about Charlie's comment, *cougar indeed. I have this one in my lair and now all I want to do is play with my food.*

He cupped her breast and noted how it made her knees sway. "I know exactly what to do. I just want to take it slow and enjoy every minute we're together. If I only get this one time with you Jana, I want it to be memorable. I'd hate to disappoint you."

"I don't think that's possible. I can't imagine that happening. Believe me this is new for both of us. Are you ready to take it to the next level?"

"Give me a few minutes and I'll be more than ready," Mike laughed. They embraced once again, Mike lifting her, taking her to the bed.

Reluctantly, Jana broke the kiss. "Mike, you realize I'm not twenty?"

"I'm very aware of the woman I'm holding in my arms."

He nibbled her neck and ran his hands up her side. "I'm not a teenager either, so don't worry about it." He felt for the hook to her bra. Mike lifted his head and looked at her, his eyes asking an unspoken question.

"What?"

Mike lifted his hands in frustration. "Where is it?"

"Where's what?"

"The hook, where is it? I know there has to be one somewhere?" Mike reached behind her and gently snapped her bra.

She laughed, "It's in the front, silly."

"I've never unfastened a bra from the front before. This is definitely a first for a lot of things."

"You've led a sheltered life young man." She teased and showed him where the hook was. She began to unhook it for him, but Mike pushed her hands away.

"Let me," he smiled. *Oh, please let me.*

"If you need any assistance, let me know." Jana lifted her hands to his face and slowly trailed them down his chest.

Mike shuddered at her touch, "You aren't making this easy."

Jana arched her eyebrows and blew him a kiss. "I never said it would be easy." She reached down and slowly ran her fingers around the waist of his briefs pushing them down around his knees and off.

Mike closed his eyes and let his head fall back. "Damn woman, do you know what you're doing?"

"I'm pretty sure I've been here before." She heard him inhale as she ran her hands down his hips and caressed his firm backside. She felt him unhook her bra and intimately stroke her breasts.

He reached down and removed her panties. "I think it's only fair that we're dressed the same."

"You aren't dressed at all."

"Exactly!" Mike begged her to leave the garter belt and stockings on. His lifelong fantasy was to make love to a woman dressed exactly this way. He couldn't remember the number of times this dream had put him to sleep. Mike's hands explored her body, feeling his way to her most sensual parts. Her nipples were erect as he massaged and caressed them. His hand moved down to her waist and dipped to her center core, slowly rubbing the nub.

"Oh Mike, that feels so good."

"Do you want me to stop?"

"Not if you want to live," she moaned.

Mike grabbed her waist and slowly pulled her atop him. Jana liked the feeling of control this position put her in. She straddled him, lowering her hips to meet his erection, allowing him to slowly enter her. *Yes, this is where I want to be, but I need to take this slow. I want this to last.*

Mike wasn't making it easy for her; his hands were everywhere: on her breasts, massaging her back and caressing her bottom. When she began to raise and lower herself enjoying the penetration, Mike lifted his head slightly to take her nipple into his mouth. He caressed a breast with one hand, while his mouth made love to the other. Jana slowed the rising and lowering of her body, releasing him from her control and then quickly impaling herself once again with each motion.

He felt his own climax build; *if I die right now the undertaker will have to cut my penis off to get it to lie down.* He stroked her nipple with his tongue, his teeth adding that small pain that hurts *so good.*

The goose bumps on Jana's body emphasized her response to Mike's touch; he definitely had her attention. At the same time she assaulted his manhood, driving it in and out of her inner core while she contracted and released with each penetration.

His arousal peaked, the exquisite heat building in his loins–up–down–up–down. Mike grabbed her hips and drove into her. He felt her tense as her orgasm built.

"Oh-God-Mike, don't stop."

Mike concentrated on each movement, feeling his cock swelling and knew he was about to shoot his load inside her love canal. "I couldn't stop if I wanted to." He met her move for move.

"Oh, yes!" Jana smiled as she also concentrated on the movement. Sex was exhilarating if it was done with the right person. It'd been a long time since she was allowed to be on top and control her pleasure. She wanted Mike to enjoy this, but *she* wanted to take charge and that's exactly what she was doing. She moved her hands up and down his chest tweaking his nipples, kissing his neck and running her tongue across his lips.

Mike was consumed by her assault. He couldn't control where she was, or what she did. He saw her smile and realized that was exactly what she wanted. *Jana needs to be in charge here just like the office. Hell if I care, I can live with it.*

Jana felt the orgasm take hold at the same time she felt Mike's release. She shuddered and collapsed. Both spent, they rolled to their sides, holding each other close sharing the intimacy of the moment. They cuddled like young lovers, closing their eyes and easing into sleep.

*****

The morning sun peeking through the blinds made her squint. Mike slowly woke, feeling her secure in his arms. He wasn't ready to release her; and to bring her even closer, as Jana snuggled into his warmth.

She was shocked, yet pleasantly surprised that they had slept through the night in each other's arms. It had been a long time since she'd spent the night with a man.

Mike massaged her back and slowly moved his hand around to caress her breast. When he brought his mouth down on hers, she yielded, the kiss consuming them. He eased her back lying between her legs with his engorged penis head pressing firmly against her swollen, moist slit.

She shifted slightly to allow him better access while keeping the contact with his body; moving her head to welcome the much desired kiss.

Mike kissed her slowly, his tongue slipping effortlessly past her lips and teeth, teasing her tongue. He used his knee to separate her legs, thrusting forward, his penis entering her.

She felt his cock jerking and shooting hot jism deep into her and they both exploded into orgasm.

They relaxed, breathing hard, but completely satisfied. They held each other closer in the afterglow.

She scratched her head, a good orgasm always made her head itch. "As much as I'm enjoying this, I need to get up and get to work. I know that isn't what you want to hear, but I've several meetings I need to get ready for." Jana leaned over, kissed him again, and sashayed to the bathroom in nothing but her garter belt and stockings, accenting her hip movements with a bit of a cat walk strut.

Her tease did exactly what she intended, he was hard as a rock and in obvious discomfort as he followed her to the bathroom. He walked in, saw her garter belt on the sink, and lovingly fingered the garment as he opened the shower door to join her.

Jana dropped the soap. "What are you doing?"

"Taking a shower."

"Really?"

"Well I was hoping you wouldn't mind taking care of a little problem I'm having." He dropped his head to his chest.

Jana followed Mike's eyes down and noticed his erection. *Oh youth, you have to love them and their stamina.* "I think I can help you with your problem, but we've got to hurry." Her eyes narrowed, "Do you know what hurry means?"

"Oh, I think so." He pressed her into the marble wall of the shower, lifting her and easing both legs around his waist so she could lock them at the ankle. He didn't hesitate, but entered her once again, beginning to move slowly, kissing her as he repeatedly penetrated her.

Mike's lips on hers sent shivers up and down her spine as he continued to plunge into her. He made love to every part of her: her mouth, nipping on the edges, using his tongue to molest her, his beautiful hands massaging her breasts, and running her nipples between his thumb and finger. His attacks on her body meshed into sheer ecstasy; and Jana cried out as she climaxed once again.

*****

Driving to the office Jana began to appreciate what a 'Cougar' was. Now that she had the definition well in hand, enjoying the freedom and power of being a Cougar was the next step. She felt sure she could do that, if last night and this morning were any indication of the satisfaction that could be realized. Yes, she knew Mike would be leaving in little more than a week, but in that time she also knew they would share as much time as they could together. Jana didn't want a husband or a boyfriend, *been there, done that.* She wanted only an intimate friend. *Okay, someone for sex.*

As she walked into the office she smiled at Charlie. "The Cougar is alive and well."

"Give, Jana." He jerked his head around and spilt his coffee.

"No, I am not going to discuss my private life with you. I do, however, want to thank you for the 'Cougar' insight. I think it's something that will work well for me." She laughed as she entered her office and closed the door.

Barely seated at her desk, Jana's intercom buzzed. *I'm not telling him anything.* "Charlie I'm not talking!"

"I'm not asking, but you have a call on line two, do you want me to take a message?"

"No, I'll take it. Who is it?"

"Craig."

"Shit, okay I'll take it." She closed her eyes and took a deep breath to compose herself. "Craig, it's good to hear from you, but I didn't think you cared for mornings?"

"You're right I don't, but I've a concern we need to talk about."

"Okay... And what would that be?"

"I saw you leave the dinner last night with that young man."

"Yes, I did. We drove over together and he gave me a lift home. Craig, his name is Mike."

There was a moment of silence and Craig came back on the line, his voice louder. "I know his name, Jana! His name is not the problem here."

"*What* exactly is the problem? Or *your* problem?"

"Do you realize the gossip that has already begun through your company and mine?"

She drummed her nails on her desk. "Actually, no, but I can guess."

"And you are not worried about our reputations?"

"*OUR* reputation?" *What is he talking about?* "Craig, let me put this as plain as I can. You can call me and talk about any interaction we have between our companies. You can call me and talk about a potential investment I might want to consider. You can call and talk to me about our daughter. But you are not allowed to call me and discuss my personal life. It is none of your business. You gave up that right two years ago, or did you forget?"

"Jana, I don't mean to put you on the defensive. I'm only concerned with you and your reputation."

"Yea, right, you are only concerned with an image you think I should maintain. Well, guess what? This is the 21st Century and women have had the right to vote, smoke and have sex at their discretion, and have had for years."

"But, Jana?"

"Don't *but* me Craig! This conversation is over; I have a lot of work to do." Jana slammed down the phone. *He has his nerve calling me. I owe him nothing, absolutely nothing. Too bad he never thought about me in our previous relationship because maybe we would still have one. Shit!* Jana reached for the intercom and buzzed Charlie. "Charlie, I'm not taking any more calls from Craig today!"

"Yes, ma'am!" *I wonder what he did or said. I bet it had to do with Mike.* Line one rang and he answered it.

"Charlie, the phone cut out, I wasn't done speaking with Jana." Craig spoke as emphatically as he could without screaming.

"Jana is not available to take your call at this time, can I take a message?"

"Charlie, I was just on the phone with her and we weren't done."

Charlie took a deep breath and mentally counted to five. "Jana is not available to take your call at this time, can I take a message?"

"This isn't funny. I need to speak with her. She's making a big mistake here and I need to stop her."

"Craig?"

"Yes?"

"Did you hear a dial tone?"

"Yes?"

"Jana is no longer available to take your calls *today*, can I take a message?" Charlie tried to be nice, but Craig wasn't getting the message.

As Charlie's unsaid meaning finally reached him, Craig mumbled, "No, no, I'll try to call her later tonight, or maybe even tomorrow. Thanks Charlie."

Charlie hung up the phone. The office grapevine probably had Jana and Mike planning a church wedding. He would take bets that marriage was not in Jana's plans. *Cougar indeed, she was definitely in charge and now even Craig knows it.*

His intercom buzzed again, "Charlie, I want you to set up dinner at the Bonefish Grill tonight, reservations for Mike and me for seven? Then please call Mike and let him know. Also tell him my car will pick him up, that way we can have drinks with dinner. Let me know if he has any problems, or if the time doesn't work for him. Okay?"

"Sure, I'll take care of it." Charlie dialed Mike's number.

"Accounting, Mike can I help you?"

"Mike, this is Charlie, Jana asked me to call and see if you were available to meet her for dinner tonight at seven."

"Sure, I don't see that as a problem. I have some things I need to take care of, but seven should work fine. I can leave from here."

"Why don't you come up to Jana's office about six-thirty and you can go over with her in the company car?"

"That won't be necessary, I can drive myself. By the way where are we going?"

Charlie laughed, "To the Bonefish Grill, Jana loves the

Pomegranate martinis they have there, as well as the food of course. She said you two would take a company car so you could have drinks with dinner, and not worry about driving afterwards."

"Okay, I guess I'm fine with that. I've got a fresh shirt and tie here so I can get cleaned up; I will need to shave. Damn I said that out loud didn't I?"

"Yes, you did. I'll let her know you are available and that you'll be presentable."

"Don't do that please. I didn't realize…"

"Mike, don't be nervous. She wants to see you and get to know you better."

"Charlie, you do know that I'm leaving the company at the end of next week, right?"

"Yes, I know and I'm sure she does too."

Mike hesitated, "Can I ask you a question?"

"Sure, and if I can I'll answer it."

"Why does she want to see me? I mean I'm twenty years younger than she is and I'm leaving in a week."

"Mike, I'm going to be honest with you. Jana's job has a lot of pressure. She very seldom lets her hair down and just enjoys the moment. Everything she's done over the past two years has been for this company, which is not a bad thing, but she needs down time. The time with you, I imagine, gives her that. Just enjoy your time together. Okay."

"Yea, thanks, good bye." Mike hung up the phone, leaned back in his chair and smiled.

Charlie buzzed Jana. "Everything is on for tonight. Mike had some work to complete so he will meet you in your office at 6:30 and you two can leave from here. Does that work?"

"Yes, that's great. Thanks Charlie." She picked up the file Mike prepared for her yesterday and reviewed it for the upcoming meeting. Even if these gentlemen came clean, she had no choice but to fire them. Stealing from her wouldn't be tolerated, whether it was chump change or millions of dollars. Who knows, maybe this new gossip, once out today, would overshadow the gossip about her and Mike. She seriously doubted it, but anything was possible. Jana walked to the bathroom to freshen up. One always wants to look her best when she has to fire someone. *The day started so well, and yet I know the next meeting and those that follow will be crap. Sometimes being boss sucks.*

Five

Jana entered the conference room, noting her staff were in their places. Long ago they'd learned the penalties of arriving late. They appeared to be in good humor, laughing and joking with each other, and discussing the past day's social event. Mike was there as well, sitting at the end of the table concentrating on the files he had brought to the meeting.

Jana took immediate control of the room. "I know you're wondering what this is all about, so I'll get right down to business. I've been reviewing our operating costs this past quarter, the costs we, you and I, have the ability to influence and control. I've concluded there are things we can do, both corporately and individually, to drive down these costs. I've identified five areas I want to concentrate on but I've decided we will address them one at a time over the next several months. Today, I want to concentrate on our travel expense accounts." She paused for a moment, and noted Daryl and Mark, her two senior managers, were looking at each other. Before she could continue Cheryl asked a question.

Cheryl furrowed her eyebrows and looked at Jana. "Are you going to take away our travel expense accounts?" Grumbling started like a virus around the table.

"No, I do, however, want each of you to take a more active

role in reviewing your staff's expense records before they are submitted to accounting for payment. Let me give you an example." The screen came to life with a slide showing a comparison of two claims. "These two examples as you can see are two travelers from separate divisions who went to the same destination. The hotel cost for these two travelers was $225 and $522 respectively. Quite a disparity, don't you think?" Jana noted that Daryl and Mark were looking at each other instead of the slide or her. "If the room for $225 meets our needs, then that's the place we instruct our staff to stay. I intend to set a standard entitlement, and set dollar limitations of what we will reimburse in the future. If someone chooses to stay somewhere else, at a different hotel, they will get only what we authorize and the remaining costs will come out of their pockets. Do any of you see this as a problem?"

Daryl took a deep breath, rising in his seat as if literally inflating his importance. "I don't have a problem. I went last month and the room I stayed in cost me $225 a night. It was nice, and there was a restaurant in the hotel which hosted a continental breakfast which was included in the room costs." He smiled, lifted his eyes and looked at Mark, suggesting he speak as well.

Mark knew he'd claimed $522 for the same room and looked down at the folder in front of him ignoring Daryl.

Jana silently bit her tongue to keep from smiling. *Asshole, you forgot the first rule of holes: when you find yourself in one, you STOP digging. Breakfast included in the room costs does not match the $17-$29 submission on your last expense record Daryl!* "The folders in front of you are the expense costs for your divisions for the past six months. I want to begin working this effort immediately, so I'll have Charlie set up individual meetings starting this morning. I want to know how you'll implement this effort. My intent is to establish a standard cost process for given areas. We will do this by area, by city, and by country. Bottom line, the less we spend, the more we make. Are there any questions?"

"What if we don't agree with this policy change?" Mark smirked and leaned forward challenging Jana's authority.

She held back her need to go for the jugular on this asshole. "I guess there are options Mark. I don't think I have to explain the obvious to anyone at this table." Jana paused as she quickly established eye contact with everyone at the table. "I'm giving you each a chance to share in this decision process, but understand me completely; I've no problem making the changes I want to see happen here."

Everyone looked around the room, but there were no comments. Jana was getting strange looks from Cheryl, but she would explain it all to her later. "Daryl, I'll start with you, but let's take ten. I'll have Charlie buzz you when I'm ready. Thanks everyone." Jana waited until everyone left the conference room, and then she turned to Charlie. "Set me up a meeting in ten minutes with Daryl. Right after he comes into my office I want you to call Mark and summon him. I want him to have to wait for me, understand? Once I'm done with those two I want to see Cheryl, but you can call her once I've finished with Mark."

Charlie watched her leave the conference room. *What's going on? She'll tell me when she's ready, I'm sure*. Back in his office he dialed Daryl on the intercom. "Jana wants to see you in ten minutes. Just have a seat in the waiting area outside her office. I have to run a quick errand, but I'll be back in plenty of time to announce you. Okay?"

"Sure, she wants to see me in ten minutes and you'll announce me. Got it. I'm assuming this is the follow-on to our meeting?" Daryl wiped the sweat from his brow.

"I can only assume it is since she didn't say anything else."

Daryl ran his hand through his tousled hair. "Okay, I'll be there. Do you know what order she is taking us in?"

"Sure, she has asked to see you, Mark and then Cheryl. Looks like seniority order to me, why?"

He relaxed—*I've got nothing to worry about*. "Just

curious, thanks." Daryl hung up and buzzed Mark. "Can you step in here a minute? I want to see you before I go see Jana."

Mark wasn't sure what Daryl's problem was, other than he was a wimp. He entered Daryl's office, "What?"

"Do you think she knows about our inflated travel claims?" Daryl wiped the sweat from his brow once again.

"That's not possible, no one knows but you and me. Get a grip!" *What an asshole.*

"Are you sure, I'm really worried. I've never done this before but you, you've been doing this for years according to the story you told me. I just know I made a terrible mistake."

"Give me a break will you?" Mark paced the room, "Just stand tall and see what she wants. Like you said, I've been doing this now for about five years, even when Craig was here. No one's ever caught me. Jana sure as hell doesn't have a clue. She's just a woman, and it amazes me she's kept this company operational since Craig left. He was the brains of this outfit. There's nothing that's changed. I looked over the numbers Mike gave us today and they didn't look out of whack to me. I don't even think the accountants saw it. Do you know who she is seeing next?"

"Yea, I asked Charlie and he said it would be you and then Cheryl."

"You mean teacher's pet didn't go first?"

"Cut it out, Mark, Jana isn't like that. If anything she's harder on Cheryl than she has ever been on us. Sorry I bothered you, I can handle this." Daryl jerked his tie to loosen it up and ran his fingers through his hair. "I'm sorry I ever let you talk me into this."

"Yea, right, like that took a lot of effort. You were a willing accomplice."

"Not as willing now as I was. If there was a way to take it back I would."

"Please, give me a break," Mark shrugged and left the office. *There is no way she knows anything; she's just a woman.*

Maybe I need to call Craig and see if he's ready to pay me what I want to join his company. I think I've let him suffer enough. Smiling, he entered his office.

Daryl reached down and picked up his planner. *What did I do with my pen? There it is.* As he reached over, he noticed that his intercom light was on. *Damn!* He was always leaving the line open, always forgetting to close the connection when he finished. *I've heard some strange things when I've left it open in the past,* he smiled. He switched it off, realizing he'd left it on after asking Mark to step into his office.

Charlie rushed to his desk, looked around to make sure Daryl hadn't arrived yet and exploded into Jana's office without knocking. "Jana you are not going to believe what I just heard!"

"Charlie, you didn't even knock. What's going on?"

"This can't wait. I need to tell you what's right under your nose. See, I had to deliver a file to Mark. He wasn't in his office so I went in and laid it on his desk. As I was leaving I heard voices." He saw Jana roll her eyes. "No, not extra-terrestrial voices, I heard Daryl and Mark talking. They were in Daryl's office; he must have left the intercom open. Anyway, I didn't mean to ease drop, but I couldn't help it. I overheard them talking about inflating their travel expenses. Daryl said something about this being the first time he did it but Mark said he'd been doing it for years even when Craig was here. I wanted you to know before you met with Daryl." Charlie finally stopped for a breath.

Jana eyes narrowed and her lips curled into a predatory grin, "Was there anything else?"

Charlie started to continue, then paused, his eyes widening as the realization swept over him. "You knew didn't you? The meeting this morning was your way of stalking your prey. You knew. Oh my God, what's going on?"

Jana silently sat back in her chair, holding an expensive Mont Blanc pen in both hands.

"You need to be careful, Mark is pissed off; I didn't understand all of his comments, but he doesn't like you; that part I'm sure," Charlie cautioned.

Jana nodded, her steady composure calming the excited Charlie. "I can't tell you any more than what you already know. I can assure you; I've got this under control."

"You've actually been stalking them haven't you? I can't believe you've been able to lull your prey into your den. They are so screwed. I love it. Okay, I'll go wait for Daryl and let you know when he gets here. This is turning out to be a very exciting day." Charlie bounced back to his desk, his body displaying the excitement he felt. When Daryl arrived he buzzed Jana. "He's here; do you want me to send him in?"

"Let him wait a few minutes. I'll buzz you when I'm ready, okay?"

"I'll take care of it." Charlie hung up the phone and turned to Daryl. "Have a seat, she's finishing up something and will be with you shortly. It shouldn't be long." Charlie watched as Daryl hesitantly took a seat and waited; he was sweating and fidgeting. Charlie couldn't help but smile with a touch of sympathy. *This man is going down.*

Both men flinched in surprise as the line to Jana's office rang. "Okay Charlie, send him in."

Charlie looked up and told Daryl that Jana would see him now.

Daryl took his handkerchief from his back pocket and wiped his face. Charlie watched him run his hands up and down his pant legs.

This guy is in serious trouble, oh well, his problem not mine. Charlie reached for the intercom dialing Mark's office. "Mark, Jana wants to see you."

There was a moment of silence, and then Mark replied, "Yea, I'll be right there."

Jana stood and came around her desk, greeting Daryl as he entered her office. *Put him at ease, then attack.* "This won't take long. I just wanted to talk to each division chief on ways they felt we could better control travel costs. I've found that a lot of the expense accounts are inflated-well, not inflated or excessive, but I'm not sure we are always taking advantage of using the corporate travel office for flights and rooms. Your division's costs, at least for this last trip, are ten percent higher. Is there a reason that you are aware of? I know you were on that trip, what do you think?"

Jana paused, allowing a heavy silence to fall over the room. "I looked over your expense record and your costs for food exceeded that of our contractors, and of Cheryl's staff. Didn't you eat together? I thought that's what I'd heard."

"Well, we did, and we didn't—I mean—there were times when I was, uh, still hungry, after the meals, so...um. I, I ordered things to take back to the room."

"So you ordered room service?"

"Well, not exactly. I actually ordered things to take with me to the room."

"Really, you were that hungry? You don't look any bigger." She smiled, shifting in her chair, making herself more comfortable, inviting a friend to friend discussion.

Daryl relaxed, noting no hostility in Jana's body language. *Maybe Mark was right, she doesn't have a clue.* "Bigger, no I actually lost weight on the trip. Some of the Asian food just doesn't agree with me."

"Why then would you order an additional meal to take to your room?" Jana's tone was concern, almost a motherly interest.

Daryl looked up, noting the concern was not motherly; it

was predatory, a stalk-and-ambush approach, and he knew she was not going to let this one go. Shaking his head in defeat, tears filled his eyes.

"What's the matter Daryl? Aren't you feeling well? Can I get you a glass of water?"

"Jana, I'm so sorry. I have a confession," he sniffed, taking his handkerchief out and wiping his eyes and nose.

"And that would be?"

"I lied." Crying harder he buried his face in his hands.

"You lied? Daryl what's going on? I don't understand. You lied about what?"

Daryl remained bent over, sobbing and shaking his head in despair. "I knew it was wrong, but I submitted my travel claim from my last trip with exaggerated food costs on it. I falsified my travel expenses. It's the only time but I did it and I'm truly sorry. I haven't been paid yet, so I guess legally I didn't commit fraud, but I did try and I'm so sorry."

Jana folded her hands and considered his answer. "Would it surprise you to know that I was aware you did this?"

Daryl's head popped up, his eyes wide with fear. "But I was told there was no way you would know."

"Really? Did Mark tell you that?"

"No, Mark, no he didn't tell me. Why-why would you think Mark would tell me something like that?"

No longer compassionate, she was now the dogged prosecutor. "Daryl, don't add complicity to your sins. Mark is involved in this isn't he? In fact I'm convinced he told you about it in one of his drunken escapades, and instead of reporting him, you decided it sounded like easy money. Am I right?"

"No, that's not true. Yes, I traveled with Mark, but we spent very little time together."

"You and Mark had a heated discussion in the bar at the hotel. What was that about?"

How could she know about that? "It wasn't about anything."

"Define anything Daryl. Remember what you say will be used against you in a court of law—yes I intend to prosecute. Tell me again, am I right about Mark?"

Daryl folded; his resolve gone. She'd broken him. He didn't intend to save Mark; hell, he wasn't even sure he could save himself. "Yes, you are. Mark has been doing this, according to his story for over five years. He told me after he had a few too many." He wrung his shaking hands and continued, "I was the only one there. I didn't realize anyone saw us. Anyway he told me it was easy and no one would know." Daryl watched Jana, waiting for her response.

"I'm really disappointed Daryl, and I'd be lying if I told you I wasn't. Since you chose this path I'll tell you what I now expect you to do." Jana rose to her feet, towering in her stilettos over Daryl as he seemed to shrink into his chair. She held out a piece of paper. "You'll sign this resignation. Once done you will leave by my back entrance. Security will meet you and assist you in clearing out your office. As of this moment you no longer work for me."

Daryl shook his head. This can't be happening. "Jana you can't fire me. I've given you over twenty years of dedicated service. This is my only mistake. Please don't do this; I have a family, a son in college."

"Daryl, first of all I'm not firing you, you're resigning. When you have time to think about it, you'll agree I'm doing you a big favor. Second, if I don't do this and the word gets out, which it will, everyone will think they can get away with stealing from this company. You really should have thought about your wife and son before you did this. To think you threw it all away for less than five hundred dollars. The good news for you, and in this I feel I'm being quite forgiving, I'm not going to prosecute you for fraud. I'm letting you walk away. I won't give you a reference, but I won't pass on what you did to another employer unless they call and ask me directly. There will be no notation on this action in your personnel records. If by chance you get another job, and the new employer asks for your history files, they will be clean. That's all I'm willing to do, and I only do that because of your wife and son and the twenty years of service." Jana walked to the door and opened it, noting the security officer waiting.

Daryl signed the resignation, dropped the pen on the desk and walked through the door.

Jana closed it behind him. *That's one down and one to go.* She walked to her desk and pushed the intercom switch, "Charlie, please send Mark in and call Detective Monroe at the number on the card I left on your desk. Let me know the minute he gets here."

Charlie looked up at Mark pacing the lobby. "Mark, she'll see you now."

"It's about damn time," he mumbled. He walked into Jana's office and took a seat in one of the wing chairs in front of her desk. "So what kind of mess do you need me to bail you out of this time? You know I didn't buy the travel expense foolishness from the meeting this morning. So come clean, what is it?"

Jana pushed her chair back, creating more space and providing her with a fuller view of her adversary. She used the trappings of power, the executive desk and furnishings to her advantage. "Excuse me, Mark, did I miss something?"

"No, YOU wanted to see ME." Calming himself, he continued, "When Craig needed to see me he always wanted me to fix something he had screwed up."

"Really? It seems you're invaluable to the organization. I never realized Craig depended on you so much."

Jana's sarcasm was lost on Mark. "Sure there were a lot of instances when he would have been in big trouble without me. So what do you want me to fix for you?"

"Actually I've no idea what you're talking about, but I don't need you to fix anything for me. The reason for this meeting is to establish travel rates for our employees. I want my manager's input before I make a final decision."

"Sure, right, okay my travel expense account. It is, and always has been, accurate to the penny. I submit it every month on time, though I have to say your accountants aren't real fast in getting the checks back to me." He leaned back, his hands behind his head. "Other than that all is well, anything else?"

Jana's eyes closed slightly as she stood, watching her prey. *Where is that detective?* "Mark, let's cut to the chase." Her intercom buzzed and she lifted the receiver. "Yes, Charlie what is it?"

"He's here; do you want me to send him in?"

"Yes, please." The door opened and Detective Monroe entered. Jana greeted him with a handshake. "Thanks for coming on such short notice."

"Not a problem, is this the gentleman you wanted me to meet?"

"Yes exactly. Mark, this is Detective Monroe. He's here to arrest your ass for the fraud you perpetrated against my company over the past five years. From the accountant's initial review, you have," she picked up a spreadsheet, "filed excessive travel expense records for over eight thousand dollars. Detective Monroe tells me that's a felony."

Detective Monroe laughed softly, "Jana, please let me have some fun here too." He removed his hand cuffs from his pocket and indicated, with his head, for Mark to stand up.

"You can't put those on me," Mark screeched.

"Actually, I can. You've committed a crime, and now you'll get a chance to request an attorney and pay your debt to society." He grasped Mark's right hand and pulled it behind him as he read him his Miranda rights. He brought the left hand back and secured the cuffs. "Let's go."

"Jana you can't let him take me out like this. I have a reputation to think about."

"Yes, that's true, we all do, but you should have thought more about yours before you did this." Her eyes never left his as she dropped the spreadsheet in the trash.

"Craig—Craig—he knew I was doing this. He never had a problem with it."

"I find that hard to believe Mark, but even if it's true, it has nothing to do with me."

"Sure it does, he was having an affair with the secretary in Purchasing while you were married, and I covered for him. He told me he would make it worth my while, but he never did, so I took care of it myself."

"Detective Monroe, can we take that as a confession?" Jana chuckled. "You know, Mark, you're the loser here. It's unfortunate Craig didn't take you with him to protect his little secret. I personally have no reason to protect you. He's all yours." Jana walked over and opened the door. "Thanks again Detective Monroe."

Mark snarled. "What about my office...my stuff?"

"Right now it's my stuff until we're done with our investigation. Let your attorney know, they can contact me direct for status. Have a good life Mark. Understand I intend to prosecute you to the full extent of the law." She turned away and ignored his further protests as the Detective pushed him out the door.

Jana walked over to her desk, sat down and leaned back in her chair. *Ten, nine, eight, seven six, five.* Her door opened and Charlie walked in. "You're getting old Charlie, it took you five seconds to get into my office, and for the second time today you didn't knock. What am I going to do with you?"

He saw the gleam in her eyes, the flush in her cheeks, the satisfaction of the stalk and kill. "Do you need me to do anything for you?"

"Yes, call Cheryl and ask her to come down. Then call Mike and ask him to stop by in about thirty minutes."

Jana had that "this isn't the time to chat" look, so Charlie followed orders. He called Cheryl and asked her to come to Jana's office as soon as she could. When she entered Jana's lobby Charlie told her she could go in.

Cheryl opened the door and entered Jana's office. *What the hell is going on? Charlie never let's anyone in without announcing them — what's going on? I know she met with Daryl and Mark.*

"Cheryl, come in and have a seat." Jana walked around the desk and took a seat facing her. "I need to let you in on some secrets."

Cheryl shook her head, "Okay."

"You know I met with Daryl and Mark already, right?"

"Yes, that was the plan you told us about from our meeting this morning."

"Well there was more to it than that. I just want you to listen to all I have to say and then I'll try to answer your questions. Daryl and Mark no longer work for me. Each in their own way have either resigned, or been terminated for cause. They both committed fraud, but only one of them walked away with money. Daryl's offense was fraud with a lot of stupidity thrown in for good measure. I let him resign." Jana paused, running her hand along her suit skirt. "Mark is another story. He committed numerous frauds over the past five years, and my intent is to prosecute him to the fullest extent of the law. What all this means to you is that you are now my Deputy Director and second in command."

Cheryl twisted her hands, her mouth opened in anticipation of Jana's next comment.

Jana continued, "I need you to get with our headhunter and see if you can identify some viable replacements for both of them as quickly as possible. The longer we delay this process the more work you and I will have to take on. If you have any ideas on potential candidates, either internal or external, I'd like to see their resume. I want your recommendations and we'll take it from there."

Cheryl couldn't help it, she fidgeted when she was excited, unprofessional as it was, and this was the best news Jana could have given her. "I'm sorry, but I think this is great. Those two have been a major pain in the ass for a couple of years. Since they joined forces in Macau they've been unbearable to work with. I'll admit I'm excited and a little scared with the position I now hold, but I'll make sure you never regret your decision."

Jana laid her hand on Cheryl's arm, "I know that. Working with you is going to be great. All that aside, can we do dinner one night next week? I think we need a ladies night out. What do you say?"

"I'm game; just tell me when and where." Cheryl leaned back in her chair, prompting a moment of silence. "I do have one question."

"Sure; anything."

"Tell me about the young stud you left the dinner with last night."

"With everything that transpired this morning that's your only question?" Jana's eyes brightened as she prepared to reveal some deep dark secret, almost purring. "Not now, he's on his way here and I need to freshen up just a little, but we can discuss it in detail over drinks, later, okay."

"Yes, that sounds great, I can't wait."

"Thanks Cheryl, now get out of here, I just gave you a lot to do and not a lot of time to make it happen. If you need anything, have a question, or just want to talk come see me. Don't let anything fester, okay."

"I'll handle it. Thanks Jana, I really do appreciate your confidence in me. Don't forget to call me for drinks when you have time."

As Cheryl left, Charlie congratulated her. He knew she was now second in command to Jana, and if one cougar was good, two were better.

Mike passed Cheryl in the lobby and offered a friendly, "Busy day?"

Her smile was one of excitement and mystery. "Like you wouldn't believe," she said.

Before he could reply Cheryl was on her way down the hall, a new bounce evident in her business pumps. He turned to Charlie. "Jana wanted to see me."

"Yes, she did. I'll announce you." Charlie buzzed Jana, "Mike's here, do you want me to send him in?"

"That would be great. Give us some time Charlie; I don't think my next meeting starts for an hour or so. Put a "Do Not Disturb" sign on the door and unless we are on fire I don't want to be disturbed, understand?"

"You got it. Mike you can go in and for your info she has about an hour then she has another meeting." Charlie glanced in the foyer and lowered his voice, "If it was me I'd lock the door behind me when I closed it, just a suggestion."

Six

An hour should be sufficient. Mike leaned back against the door to lock it as it closed.

Jana's head jerked at the slight click of the lock. "Did you lock my door?"

"Yes, I did. Is that a problem?"

"No, I guess not," she leaned back in her chair, "if Charlie needs me he can buzz me on the intercom."

"He won't need you for at least an hour."

Jana licked her lips, consciously or unconsciously, she didn't know. "And you know this... How?"

"He told me when he said I could come in without knocking."

"He's getting rather liberal with my privacy. Is there something you need?"

"Need, no, want…desire…lust after, yes."

Jana's face paled from the comment. "You can't be serious; this is a place of business."

"We are both well aware of that, but the way I see it...you have some free time right now and need to wind down...and I have some free time too, so we should spend some of that free time taking care of each other."

"Really, one night of—"

"Wait, it was one night and one morning."

"Okay, one night and one morning," she couldn't keep the smile from her face, "does not give you the right to walk into my office and keep me from my work."

"You're right. The real reason I'm here is to ask if I can take you away from all of this."

"You mean away from the office? What are you talking about? Did I miss something?"

"Let me start again." He patted his suit coat. "I have in my left breast pocket two tickets to Las Vegas, leaving tomorrow afternoon. I would like you to go with me and spend the weekend. We can play tourist. I have a little work to do with my Uncle, but other than that my time will be free. We can stay with my aunt and uncle."

Jana reclined in her executive chair and warily eyed him. "Wait just a minute, you want me to drop everything and leave with you tomorrow for Las Vegas for the weekend, you already bought the tickets and have it all planned out? Your Aunt and Uncle?"

"Yea, uh...well, I bought tickets so my brother and I could fly out there for the weekend and do some bonding while I got a few things straightened out for my business venture. He called this morning and he has a business trip he can't get out of, so I have an extra ticket. I called the airline and I can change the ticket to your name. Will you go with me to Las Vegas for the weekend?" He saw her mind working.

Her head fell back and her eyes closed. There was a moment of silence and then she placed her hands flat on her desk. "You know what, yes I will go."

"That's great! We leave at three-fifteen tomorrow. We can just play tourist if that works for you."

"It does, with one slight change. I'm not staying with your aunt and uncle. I'll call Sam at the Venetian and see if we can get a room on short notice. He's always helped me in the past and maybe, just maybe, we can get the rooms for nothing."

"That would be great, but it isn't necessary."

"Look, Mike, if I go I want to stay at the Venetian, take it or leave it."

"Oh, I'll definitely take it. Call your friend Sam," Mike reluctantly agreed.

"Sam's not a friend. He's a Player Development Representative for the hotel."

"I'll bite, what exactly is that?"

"Basically because I go to Las Vegas regularly, and I stay at the Venetian, they get a lot of my playing dollars; I love to play the slots. Anyway I get a lot of offers to stay there up to three nights for free, and I take advantage of them when I can. Let me call Sam and see what he can do?"

As Jana made the call Mike walked around the office taking in the collection of little boxes she had. They were very ornate. *I need to ask Charlie about these. I want to get her something to remember our time together; maybe something like this would be good.* As he picked up one of the boxes something rattled inside. *Jelly beans; is this some type of joke?* He set down one box and picked up another, and sure enough there were six jelly beans inside. *Something else I need to ask Charlie about.*

"Sam, this is Jana Gates, I hate to bother you but I'm wondering if it would be possible to get a room, king size bed, non-smoking, for three nights beginning tomorrow. I know it's late but I really hope you can help me."

"Jana, it's good to hear from you again, let me check. We have a convention in town, but let me see if we have any cancellations."

Jana could hear the typing of the keyboard in the background. *I hope he can make this happen, it would make a great trip for Mike and me*, and she longingly sighed for concurrence of her plan.

"We can accommodate you for the three nights. Will you be traveling alone?"

"No, I'll have a friend with me. Thanks, Sam I really appreciate your help on this. I do have a couple of small favors to ask though."

"Sure, whatever I can do to help."

"Will you see if you can get us two tickets to the Phantom, Gold Circle center seats, for Friday night and dinner reservations at Delmonico Steakhouse for 9:30 p.m.? If you can make those two things happen just include the details in your e-mail with my room confirmation number."

"Do you want me use the credit card I have on file?"

"Yes, and Sam, thanks again for everything." Hanging up the phone she turned and saw Mike standing by the window, his shoulders slumped.. "What's wrong?"

"Jana, I didn't want you to take me to Las Vegas, I wanted to take you."

"You *are* taking me, you got the tickets."

"True, but you're making it a vacation experience."

"No, what I'm doing is what I always do when I go to Vegas. Mike, please just go with me and enjoy yourself. It'll be fun. We can sleep in, enjoy the big tub in the bathroom, or play in the shower, they have both and they are big enough for two people." Her eyes twinkled at the thought of her and Mike in that multi-head marble shower.

"But, Jana, it's not right. I should be paying for this trip, not you. You're my guest."

"Tell you what, you put that male ego in your pocket and we can make this trip. If not, I won't go and you and your ego can have a good time—alone."

Mike reached out, pulled her into his arms and kissed her. His tongue explored the inner recesses of her mouth, tasting a unique licorice taste, even though he didn't make the connection between it and the contents of the little boxes around her office. He continued to nibble on her lips, her chin and down her neck.

Opening her silk blouse, he felt the lace of her bra and smiled. "I've got the panties that go with this bra."

She stepped back, "You've got what?"

"I've got the panties that match this lovely bra."

"That actually explains a lot." She laughed as she remembered how confused she'd been that morning when she'd thought she'd taken both from her lingerie drawer. "I thought I was having a senior moment. I put out my clothes this morning and I couldn't find the panties anywhere. I finally picked another pair from the drawer. How'd you do that?" She pointed her finger at the panties with a 'how could you' look.

"Like you said, you laid them on the bed and as I was leaving I picked them up and put them in my pocket." His boyish grin continued as he pulled the panties from his pocket.

Jana reached for them. "Give me those."

"No, you can't have them, at least not yet."

"They're mine. What do you mean I can't have them, yet?" They were both laughing now.

"I want to put them on you, and I didn't have time this morning."

"Mike, I have panties on, thank you very much." She reached down and began buttoning her blouse.

"Not so fast. I want to make love to you, here, now, and when we're done I'll put these panties on you, and I'll take the ones you have on with me."

Jana placed her hands on her hips and stomped her foot. "This is my office! We're not going to make love in here."

"Yes, we are, right here, right now." Mike backed her into her desk and slowly lifted her, balancing her on his leg and the edge of the desk. He kissed her again, removing her jacket and blouse at the same time. With unbridled lust he kissed her breasts through the lace as Jana steadied herself on the desk. He kissed down her body, slowly working her skirt up around her waist. She couldn't resist yielding to his passion.

He gently pulled down her panties leaving them dangling from her ankle. Parting her nether lips with his fingers he was intoxicated by her womanly musk.

Jana tried to move away, but her struggle only enhanced the contact as she slid from the desk top forcing his face closer to her nexus of desire.

Mike kissed his way back to her hips. As he rose he unhooked the bra, licking, sucking and repeatedly arousing her nipples with his teeth.

She inhaled deeply as he moved from side to side. Jana leaned forward reaching for his belt, unzipping his pants, letting them fall to the carpet. The briefs, though still on did not impede his erection which was already exposed. He was more than ready for her.

Jana moved forward as his hands braced her backside and he entered her in one easy motion. She was ready and within seconds she climaxed, tightening her legs around his waist.

Feeling their mutual heat, Mike moved faster, increasing the friction between them.

She cried out as Mike erupted, exploding both mentally and physically. Jana fell forward onto his chest as he held her close.

Mike leaned back, taking a hard look at the woman he'd just made love to. *This woman was phenomenal. She is sexy, stimulating and I can't get enough of her.* "Do you want me to put your matching panties on you now?" he pleaded.

"Yes, but not just yet, let me clean up first." She started to walk toward the bathroom and Mike stopped her.

"No, you relax in your chair and I'll get a damp cloth; I'll be right back."

Jana closed her eyes and let her head fall back, completely satisfied. *I just made love in my office with a young, good looking, accountant.* She smiled. *I can't believe I just did that. I wonder if he can do it again, now.*

Mike walked back into the office and knelt before her. "Allow me, please."

"Okay," she murmured as Mike wiped the love juices from between her legs with the warm cloth.

"Thank you." Mike took the peach panties out of his pocket and helped her put them on. He stood, bringing her out of the chair and into his arms. "That was fantastic. You *are* the sexiest woman I've ever met. Our hour is almost up and before Charlie breaks down the door I need to finish dressing and let you get back to work. I'll meet you here at six-thirty so we can go to dinner."

She purred, "Yes, I'll see you then." Jana was astounded. *In all of my life I've never made love in my office, but I definitely need to do it more. What a therapeutic relaxer. Wow!* She watched Mike walk to the door twirling her discarded satin panties in his left hand. He held them to his nose inhaling her scent and then placed them in his suit pocket as he opened the door whistling, off key. Laughing, she directed her concentration back to her job, retrieving the file she needed for her next meeting. *Okay, fun's over, back to work.*

Mike stopped by Charlie's desk once again. He looked around, ensured they were alone and whispered. "I've got another question?"

"Shoot, but hurry I need to get her to the next meeting."

"What are the little black beans in those boxes in her office? What's up with that?"

Charlie laughed, "Jelly Bellies, licorice Jelly Bellies, she craves them. She doesn't obsess about them, but when she's nervous you'll see her put two or three in her mouth. She loves them, and yes they make her physically ill at times if she eats too many, but she loves them. Why?"

"I noticed them in a couple of the boxes, and though I thought they were jelly beans I couldn't figure out why they were there. It reminds me of a squirrel storing nuts."

"I guess it could be perceived that way, but I'm actually the one who puts them in all the little containers. She knows they're in there, and once in a while I'll find them empty and refill them. She has a stash in her desk drawer, and I know she keeps them at her house too. Is everything okay with her?"

"We didn't discuss this morning's events, but I think she's fine. She's relaxed and our talk was exactly what she needed," Mike stared at her door.

"That's good news, as her next meeting, based on the rumor mill, won't go any better. She's meeting with your replacement."

Mike shrugged, "I've tried to give him some pointers, but he isn't listening. She can handle him without a doubt. Take care."

"Again, thanks for being there for her, she needed some down time." At least Charlie hoped it was down time. Mike appeared to be relaxed and he hoped Jana was in the same state of mind.

Charlie remembered to knock, waited a few seconds, and then entered her office. Nothing seemed out of the ordinary. Jana was sitting at her desk reviewing the proposal Sean had sent up. "What do you think of Sean's recommendations?"

"Can't say I'm surprised, but it's not what I want. I'll have to get him to adjust his way of thinking or I'll call his boss and ask for a replacement."

"Cheryl's secretary said all parties were in the conference room waiting for you. Are you ready?"

"Sure, join me on this one. Follow my lead, okay."

"Not a problem." Charlie followed her into the conference room. *Oh no! That idiot is sitting in Jana's chair. Has he lost his mind?* Charlie waited, watching her take another seat at the table.

Jana noticed Sean in her chair and she didn't skip a beat. She sat down next to Cheryl, and Charlie took the seat next to her. Sean looked at Cheryl, "Is everyone here?"

"Yes, everyone's here," Cheryl looked at Jana who

nodded to get the meeting started. *I love it when she breaks in a newbie.*

"I guess the boss isn't going to make it, so let's get started. For those of you I've not met, my name is Sean Bisbee. I'm taking Mike's place and I wanted an opportunity to lay some ground rules on where we go from here." He noticed the blonde to his right. *Very pretty, a little old for my taste, but very pretty.* "From the reports I've reviewed you aren't using enough accounting information to make valid decisions. Seems to me, and this is nothing against Mike, but it appears there have been some short cuts taken that need to be rectified immediately. The folders in front of you lay out my plan, and as of right now these are the reports you will receive."

Jana grimaced. *Another accountant who's only training was from a textbook and who has no idea that companies today need more than lag indicator information. I'll just let him continue to dig his own hole.*

"Are there any questions?"

Jana touched Cheryl's leg under the table, indicating she wanted her to ask questions. "Sean, what's wrong with what we're getting today? That information has been very helpful in projecting my needs of people and finances."

"That's true, but you can get the same info by running some standard ratio comparisons on the financial statements I've provided."

"I don't want to have to do that. I want that information readily available and the reports Mike set up do exactly that. I don't have to do any additional calculations. I can also break it down by each of my branches and by individual. The financial statements are at too high a level for me, our boss needs that info from a corporate perspective, but I don't. If you want my opinion, the reports we get now are exactly what we need." The other division chiefs all nodded in agreement.

"That isn't standard accounting practice and based on the

services my company provides that is what the 'Statement of Work' calls for, nothing more."

Again, Cheryl chimed in, disbelieving his last comment, "You're saying you don't intend to provide this information in the future because it's not in your contract?"

"That's correct. I see no flexibility in this area, and though I haven't discussed it with Mr. Nixon, I'm sure he'd agree."

"Young man," Jana's mouth tightened with each word. "I assure you Mr. Nixon knows exactly what Mike was providing, and is in full agreement that it fits within the contract scope."

"No, I'm sure he doesn't, as his direction to me, when he gave me this job, was how important standardization was to controlling costs, and that this company was concerned with rising costs and wanted them cut."

Jana stared down the young accountant. "Do you know everyone in this room?"

"Well no, I haven't had time to meet everyone."

Jana nodded, "Okay, fair enough, let's take a few minutes to introduce ourselves so Sean knows who is responsible for what. Cheryl, go ahead and start." The division chief's introduced themselves, identifying their work and what they did to support the company. Lastly, Jana stood, walking to the head of the table where Sean was seated. "I, young man," she emphasized each syllable, "am Jana Gates, CEO for this company and your bill payer. You are in my seat. MOVE!"

Sean stumbled from his seat and fell into the one Jana had vacated. "M-m-Ma'am, I didn't mean any disrespect. I'm just trying to save this company some money."

"Really, that was your objective here? Actually I'm somewhat surprised. Did you just get out of school Sean, or are you coming to us from a previous employer?"

"No, yes, I graduated from school a couple of months ago, tested and obtained my CPA credentials almost simultaneously, but have been working as an accountant for quite some time for the company I work for now."

"Have you ever worked inside a company you supported, like you're planning to do now?"

"No, I've only provided financial reports to the companies we've worked for."

"That's what I thought. I'm going to lay it out for you very carefully. In this company I call the shots. In this company the reports Mike specifically designed for my management's use are exactly what I want and what I'm willing to pay for. The financial reports you have included in these folders are for my use only, most of my staff, excluding Charlie, never see them. I would, however, like you to start sending all to Cheryl as she is my next in command, effective immediately. All that said; do we understand each other?"

"Yes, I think so. You want the reports Mike designed for your division heads and the full financial reports should be provided to you and Cheryl once a month."

"No weekly, monthly, quarterly and as needed."

"Yes, as needed, anything else?" he desperately wanted out of the room and to be alone.

"No, that's all. I hope you've learned a valuable meeting lesson today-know your audience." Jana left the room.

Sean leaned to Charlie, "She's a tough one." he whispered. *That last look she gave me was the kind of expression one might see on the face of a cat. But there would invariably be feathers involved,* he cringed.

Charlie smiled, "You don't know the half of it. She was actually gentle, by some standards." Charlie noticed beads of perspiration on Sean's lip and forehead. *So young and so stupid, he'll learn, unfortunately the hard way it seems.*

Seven

As Jana changed into a light, linen summer dress, she couldn't stop the day's activities from running through her mind. Firing folks was not her forte. The intercom buzzed again. *I hate that thing.* "Yes, Charlie."

"Craig's on the line, he says it's important."

"That's what he always says, but I'll take it," she grimaced.

"Craig, two calls in the same day, people are going to talk."

"I know you've had a rough day, and I appreciate you taking the time to talk to me. I wanted to tell you I'd hired Daryl. I didn't want you to hear it from someone else."

"That was quick, but it begs the question, why? Why would you want to hire someone without the balls to do what is ethically correct? Or one that was so easily led down the primrose path by slime like Mark?"

"Daryl is different. He made a mistake, and since you hadn't paid him yet fraud was not exactly perpetrated."

"I wouldn't take that one to the bank if I was you, but your company is your business. Let me make something perfectly clear though. My company will have no dealings with Daryl. If that happens, even once, I'll take my business elsewhere. Do I make myself perfectly clear?"

"I understand and it won't be a problem."

"Better not be."

"Jana, I also want to apologize for the call this morning. You're right, your personal life is none of my business."

Jana wasn't going to fall for that ploy, "If there's nothing else, I'm getting ready to leave for the day, I have dinner plans."

"One more thing, I got a call from Detective Monroe; he wants to talk to me about Mark. Monroe said Mark told you I was having an affair with one of our employees."

"That's not important Craig; you no longer owe me any explanations."

"Agree, but I wanted you to know Mark was lying. I told Monroe that as well. It never happened. Monroe also asked me to pass on, though I think he said he left a message on your voice mail, that Mark is out on bail and you should be careful. Mark is angry."

"Thanks Craig, I'm glad it wasn't true. I didn't believe him, but you never know. As for Mark, I'll be careful, take care Craig," Jana hesitated as she hung up the phone. She was glad he hadn't had an affair, but it didn't really matter anymore. Running a comb through her hair, fluffing it here and there with her fingers, she walked out of her office and met Mike as he entered her foyer. "I hope you're hungry because I'm starved." Linking her arm in his, she waved good-bye to Charlie. As they approached the waiting Lincoln Town Car, the chauffer opened the back door for them. Jana slid across the seat to the middle and snuggled next to Mike. He put his arm around her and held her close. "I know you've had a rough day, so let's not talk about work, let's just enjoy the evening."

"I'm all for that. The Bonefish Grill, please Steven." Raising the window between the seats to allow her and Mike privacy, she turned and nibbled on his lips. "I've missed you."

Mike couldn't believe how natural all this felt. He moved his hand slowly under her dress, caressing her thigh and working his fingers into her wetness. Jana nibbled on his neck as he moved one finger, then two, then three into her. He felt her climax building, and he matched stroke for stroke with the intensity of her shifting hips as she met him. Jana shuddered and Mike was amazed to find that after she came so powerfully and thoroughly she didn't need to stop and rest. It was like defying gravity.

She smiled at him and began making love to his mouth, leading their tongues into an intimate tango as she unzipped his pants, stroking his erection. Mike moaned as she continued to run her hand up and down his length. Jana leaned down and ran her tongue along his engorged member. She licked, nibbled, and sucked with precision, knowing exactly what to do.

Mike moaned. *Oral sex, in the back of a limo, with a vivacious woman, my date, oh God, I'm going to come.* Jana felt his climax and as he came she licked every drop from his manhood. "That was the ultimate," he whispered.

"Just consider it an appetizer," she smiled as she sat upright, took out a breath mint and popped it in her mouth.

Mike was entranced as she freshened her lipstick, watching her apply the creamy red coloring to her full lips. He imagined the touch of her lips across the tip of his cock as she brushed her lips back and forth to evenly spread the color. When she licked her lips to add an additional sheen it was almost his undoing. *I never thought a woman putting on lipstick was erotic, man was I ever wrong.* He stifled a groan as he attempted once again to squelch the desire building between his legs.

As the limo pulled to the curb, Steven hurried around and opened the door, smiling at Jana when she exited. "Give me a call, Ma'am, when you're ready to go, I'll be close by."

"Thank you, Steven, please get something to eat as we'll be a couple of hours I'm sure."

As Jana and Mike walked into the restaurant, Mike informed the hostess that they had reservations and within seconds they were led to a private, secluded corner booth. "Thanks, I couldn't have done better myself," he said as he pressed a ten spot into her palm. The waiter immediately approached the table and without hesitation Mike ordered Jana a Pomegranate martini and himself a beer.

She reached across the table and pressed her hand to his. "You got that down quick," Jana laughed. "I was married for thirty plus years, and no matter where we went for dinner I always had to order my own drink. Granted it has only been recently that I've taken to drinking martinis, but still, it's nice that you knew what I drink. But how do you know, since we've never been to dinner before tonight?"

Mike grinned, "I asked Charlie what you liked to drink." The waiter asked what they wanted for dinner and again Mike ordered an appetizer and dinner for both of them.

"I'm impressed," Jana said, "and did your pre-date reconnaisance include my favorite meals?"

"Charlie told me you really prefer fried fish better than grilled, but that you really liked their Coconut Crusted Shrimp appetizer and their Alaskan Halibut with breading on it. I called earlier and arranged to have both ready when we got here."

"He's right about that. I think it's my Midwest upbringing. I do like fried foods, and fish is no different. Here they do some nice breading, and I've found that I prefer it to the heavier fried selections I normally ask for." Over dinner they talked about everything and nothing, enjoying each other's company, more drinks and ultimately shared a dessert of Crème Brule.

It was a nice evening with a young lover, and Jana was enjoying herself immensely. The ride over hadn't been bad either she smiled to herself. *I don't usually perform oral sex; although I certainly don't mind it being performed on me. Mike seemed to like it, at least he didn't complain. He was satisfied, and he's brought out the bolder parts of my sexual nature.* "You're welcome to spend the night with me if you like," Jana lifted her eyes waiting for Mike's response.

"I can't, not tonight. I promised my mom I'd stop by. I have some stuff in my car I need her to hold until I get a place in

Las Vegas and she can ship the boxes to me. They are leaving in the morning and won't be back before I leave. You could come with me, and then I could take you home," he suggested.

"No, I don't think that's a good idea, taking me home to meet your mom and dad probably wouldn't be easily understood." She laughed at the thought. "Hell I'm not sure I'd understand it. Let's call it a night and I'll meet you tomorrow at noon, my office. Bring your suitcase and we'll leave from there for the airport and our Vegas get away."

"Sounds like a plan," Mike said. "I'll take a cab back to the office to get my car. You can take the limo and go on home, that way you don't have to go out of your way to drop me off."

"It's not out of the way," Jana smiled, "I was hoping we could continue our little discussion in the car."

"Jana, you're killing me," Mike moaned

Jana laughed, "Allow me to make an executive decision. Leave your car in the parking garage; your stuff is safe there. Tomorrow you and Charlie can bring the boxes upstairs to my office and put them in the storeroom. When you're ready for them Charlie will send them to you. How does that sound?"

"Are you sure? I don't want to put you or Charlie out. I *would* like to be with you tonight but I don't want to impose."

"I wouldn't have suggested it if I wasn't willing. Call your folks and tell them you've made other plans and wish them a safe trip. Then join me for the evening. Remember our days together are ticking by and I really would hate to miss out on any opportunities that are available to us."

Mike dialed his parent's home and Jana listened to the one sided conversation. "Mom, I'm not going to bring the boxes by—my boss says they'll store and ship them for me when I get my place—No it's not a problem for them; it's part of their service." He smiled shyly. "Sure mom— I'll be sure and thank them. You and dad have a safe trip. Give me a call when you get back. Yes same cell phone number. Love you too, bye." He smiled at Jana. "It wasn't exactly a lie."

"No, it wasn't and I'm glad I've been able to lure you into my den for yet another night of sex and debauchery." His face turned bright red as she laughed and hugged him. "You are priceless, let's get the hell out of here."

The ride to Jana's condo was quiet and uneventful, even though she had alluded to more. Yes, she'd draped her legs over his and yes, he'd been massaging and playing with her thigh, but in actuality she'd made no further advances, and he had opted to go along for the ride refraining from further intimacy. They relaxed together and enjoyed the forty-minute ride to her condo in quiet. Every once in a while she would lean over and kiss him, or let him kiss her. Mike hurt, he was swollen and he was sure she knew it, as she seemed to shift her legs just enough to brush his manhood, making it throb even more. Steven informed them the condo was coming up and Jana shifted her legs to the front of the seat. She leaned over and kissed, massaging his erection and making it harder, if that was possible. He whimpered and she placed her finger on his lips, "I'll take care of this very soon now."

"God, I hope so," he whined.

Jana thanked Steven for his services and she walked directly in front of Mike as they entered the condo, preventing anyone from seeing his obvious erection. She unlocked the door and before he could close it she attacked. "You've fed me, you've let me rest, and now I need sex, pure unadulterated sex. Can you handle that?"

"Without a doubt." He lifted her into his arms and carried her to the bedroom, tossing her on the bed.

Jana began to remove her dress, "Bet I can get naked before you do." But she was wrong, Mike was already naked and she'd missed the whole thing. "Can we at least turn down the bed?"

"Okay, but you better hurry or I won't be responsible."

Jana threw the coverlet back in one swing, easing onto the bed as Mike joined her. "I didn't think we'd ever make it. God, I've missed this." She eased her body next to his, allowing his erection to fill her.

There was no foreplay; they'd been doing that since they got in the car. He needed to be inside her, to feel her climax around him. Jana took his tongue in her mouth, lavishly circling it with her own. He liked what she was doing, liked it so much he felt a further stirring in his loins, and he automatically reached out to caress her face. He placed his hand on her breast, touching the softness, making small circles around the hardened nipple. Jana was moaning as Mike slid his erection into the folds of her sex. She was so wet and ready he couldn't believe it. She shuddered as she reached her climax, exploding over and over in a series of orgasms. He held her close and waited for the tremors to subside. Mike had never felt such release from a woman. Before he could finish his climax he felt Jana reach another orgasm, rocking her body from head to toe. Totally spent, they collapsed in each other's arms.

As Jana eased into a quasi sleep Mike continued to massage and kiss her body. He nibbled on her neck and felt her move closer to him, encouraging his contact. Mewing, she wrapped her arms around him massaging his back, neck, and running her fingers through his hair. Mike moved to her silk heat, inhaling the smell of sex that rose from her. As Mike kissed and licked her female lips Jana opened her legs further. Oral sex, the ability to bring a woman to orgasm with his mouth alone was one of his biggest fantasies; he hoped he was doing it right. Jana moved his head slightly to the left and up just a bit, giving him encouragement as she urged him on. She moaned as Mike brought his hands up to fondle her breasts while his mouth devoured her sex. Her sexual pleasure was his goal, and he felt he was close. The stimulation of her breast seemed to be helping.

"Yes, yes, don't stop, please don't stop," she purred.

Mike felt like he was in control, in charge, he could actually understand how Jana felt when she was on top. He was erect once again, and once she reached her peak, which he knew was approaching he intended to take it to the next level. Jana shuddered down to her toes, not once, not twice but three times. She began to relax, but Mike moved up quickly capturing her legs and hooking them around his waist as he lifted her and placed her on his erection. Jana's eyes opened in shock, but she smiled and began to move with him. Their mouths met and again their tongues became serpents of passion and desire. Close to climax, Mike pounded into her, forcing her to cling to him. Jana began to orgasm and they peaked together. "Jana that was unbelievable. I can't seem to get enough of you."

"Since I don't plan to go anywhere in the near future, partly because I am physically exhausted, just wake me when you're ready to go again. I'm pretty sure I can keep up." She smiled as she nestled into him, relaxing her legs, leaving him inside her as she lulled to sleep.

"Jana?" Mike whispered.

"Yes, love."

"What kind of sheets are these?"

She opened her eyes to see if he was serious. "Sheets? Are you serious?" *We just had earth shaking, over-the-top sex and he wants to know what kind of sheets I have?* "They're thousand count Egyptian cotton sheets; almost satin in texture, but they're cooler to sleep on than satin, at least in my opinion." She scrunched her eyes, trying to focus on Mike.

"If you remember, tomorrow will you tell me where you get them?" Mikes's hand stroked the sheet between them. " They're the softest things I've ever slept on, and something I definitely want for my new apartment."

"Okay, yea, tomorrow." *This young man is amazing, and just downright cute. He fucks my brains out, and then wants to shop for sheets.* For a second night they blissfully fell asleep in each other's arms.

Jana woke to the ringing phone. "Yes, hello, whoever the hell it is, and it better be good."

"Jana, this is Charlie."

Startled, she sat up in bed; fully awake. "Charlie, what's the matter," She looked at the clock; it was four a.m. and she knew something was wrong.

"Are you alone, Jana?"

"Um—not exactly, what's up, what's wrong, tell me."

"It's Mark, Jana. He blew his brains out. He left a suicide note saying he couldn't live with what he'd done to the company, to you, or to his family. He even apologized to Craig for lying."

"Shit! Shit! Shit!" She looked at the clock again. "How'd you hear about this, at this time of night?"

"Detective Monroe was trying to get in touch with you and the switchboard directed his call to me. I advised him I'd call you and let you know. He also called Craig. Oh, there's something else."

"Holy shit Charlie, what else could there be?"

"I guess before Mark got drunk and decided to do himself in, he broke into the parking garage and defaced both your car and Mike's. He broke out headlights, slashed tires; you know normal juvenile delinquent stuff."

"Damn! I should've known that man had no balls. Shit, shit, shit! Fuck, I hate when they can't stand up to me face to face and instead take it out on something I love or someone I love. Okay Charlie, I'd appreciate it if you would deal with that personally. There are some boxes in Mike's car that need to be moved upstairs and then you can send his car and mine in for repairs."

At the mention of his name Mike turned over and rubbed his eyes, "What was that about my car?"

"Thanks Charlie, see you in a couple of hours." She hung

up the phone and turned to Mike. "Sorry, Mark vandalized our cars before he shot himself early this morning."

"He did what? Jana, what about his family? Maybe we should cancel our trip to Vegas so we can deal with this. I really need to have that car fixed so I can leave next week."

"It's under control; I'm handling it. I'll call Craig in the morning and see if there is anything we can do for Mark's family. He was closer to Mark and his wife than I ever was. As for your car, don't worry about it; Charlie will take care of it straight away. The repairs will be paid for by my Company since your vehicle was in the company lot." Jana sighed, her body shrinking as the weight of the events descended on her. "Now let's go back to sleep."

As she eased back into their spoon sleeping arrangement, Jana realized Mike had another erection. *A woman's work is never done;* she rolled over and kissed her very alert, very sexy, very much in need of satisfaction lover. Jana pushed him back as she climbed on his lap one more time. *God this feels good, I've been denying myself this for far too long.* She moved up and down, rotating her hips in sync with Mike's movements. He caressed her breasts, reaching up to kiss each in turn. Their climax built, and Jana cried out as she orgasmed; but she didn't stop until she felt Mike's release. She slithered down, releasing his swollen shaft from her female clutches and rolled in behind him. She placed her hand around his waist and gently stroked him.

"If you don't stop that we aren't going to get any more sleep."

"Okay," her tongue flicked at his ear, "I'll stop, with the understanding that this weekend is sex, sex, a little gambling, some probably much needed food, and more sex. Do you agree?" She squeezed him slightly and waited for him to answer.

"Yes, ma'am I'm here to please, and please, and please," he whispered as he drifted off to sleep.

Jana soon joined him, her hand clutching her prize.

Eight

The company car left Mark's house, as Jana and Mike relaxed in the back seat. They'd met Craig and talked to Mark's wife, who seemed to be holding up well, with family around her. Losing Mark didn't seem as traumatic as Jana had expected it would be. In fact, his wife seemed to accept the path she and her children would begin.

Back at her office she relaxed in her chair and closed her eyes. The fact that she and Mike were getting away for the weekend was a God send; she definitely needed the down time. She dialed Mike's intercom. "Hi handsome, do you know what your schedule is for the weekend? I'd like to do some planning of my free time if possible."

"Good of you to check in," he responded professionally. "Yes, I can answer that. I have a meeting Saturday that starts at ten, and will probably last a good portion of the afternoon. After that I'll be free for the remainder of my visit. Does that work?"

"It does, I take it you aren't alone, so I won't keep you. Hope you brought some dress clothes as we have a dress up evening ahead. The rest of the weekend will be casual. My car will take us to the airport so meet me in the lobby at noon and we'll leave from there. I got a message from Sam at the Venetian and he's taken care of everything. I'm going to give him a quick call and see if he can get me into the spa tomorrow while you're in your meetings. See you in about an hour."

Mike set the receiver down and finished briefing Sean on the types of reports Jana's management team expected daily, weekly and monthly. He questioned Sean on his first meeting with senior management, even though he already knew. "So Sean did everything go alright with the CEO yesterday?"

"Not exactly; I guess the good news is that I'm not a eunuch. She's a tough one, but I'm pretty sure I can handle her. She'll come around to my way of thinking in time."

Mike shook his head. "Sean, I hate to disappoint you, but if you don't come around to *her* way of thinking soon, your time here will be short. Based on what I heard yesterday, if you don't get your shit together she'll have your balls. She takes no prisoners. You obviously missed her telling you exactly what she wanted and what she expected you to provide to her. If you doubt she was telling you the truth you are dead wrong. Do what she says; get her forecasting information from the financial statements and you'll be her new best friend. Screw with her and continue to believe you have all the answers and she'll have you fired, guaranteed. I hate to remind you of this, but you're a contractor and thus dispensable." He knew Sean wasn't paying attention. As part of his departure interview with Mr. Nixon next week he would apprise him of the situation so he could do damage control. Sean left Mike's office cocky as ever. *That boy is in for a rude of awakening. His problem not mine, I warned him.* Mike finished the two reports for Cheryl and forwarded them to her e-mail. He changed out of his suit, and put on a comfortable pair of tight fitting jeans and a bright colored polo shirt, elegant in his mind but still casual. He arrived in the lobby only minutes before Jana.

Jana stepped from the elevator dressed in an orange suede jacket and cropped pants. She approached Mike and held out her hand, which he took reluctantly, afraid of what on-lookers would say. "Don't worry about it. If we give them fodder for their gossip they leave other poor souls alone." She kissed him on the cheek. "Let's get out of here." The driver picked up her two off-white Samsonite Black Label Alexander McQueen suitcases.

"Are you planning on staying longer than the weekend?" Mike compared her two bags to his single carry on.

"No silly," she touched his cheek, "just the weekend. I like to travel prepared, and when you have to pack for both casual and dress, I find two separate bags work best."

"I do like the way you look," Mike said."You're always so put together. The shoes, the bag, even the jacket all say..."

"The term would be casual, but elegant," Jana said.

Mike's eyes took her in, from her high heels to her perfectly coiffed hair, "Yea, exactly, yea."

Jana slid across the leather seat, inhaling the rich smell of the leather and the luxury of the seats. She noticed how well Mike filled out his jeans. The suits she normally saw him in didn't do justice to his shapely behind and the flatness of his stomach. She hadn't really had a lot of time to enjoy those aspects of her young paramour, and she was really hoping this weekend would give her that opportunity.

Steven turned from the front seat, "Do we need to make any stops on the way to the airport?"

"No, we're good." Mike and Jana answered, and then laughed. They'd only been together a few days and already they were thinking alike.

"Sit back, relax, I'll have you there within the hour." Steven responded. "Your flight is on schedule at last check, and you should have plenty of time to get through security." He closed the window between the seats.

Mike looked at Jana's purse and laughed. "You know, that's going to set off the alarms in the airport with all those buckles and chains."

"The good news is that it goes through the security scanner without a problem. I like to give the TSA guys something to do versus just standing around. I do love the new Ralph Lauren collection though." She raised her foot and teasingly wiggled it, "I really love the sandals with the Lucite heels and the snakeskin tote."

"You are really something." Mike shook his head. "How do you have time for all this? To me it's a purse and shoes."

Jana looked at him in mock horror.

"Okay," Mike held up a hand in surrender, "it's more than that, but most people who look at you see only a purse and shoes. They don't know the difference; I'm sure."

"That's where you're wrong. Most woman notice and I can also guarantee you they can tell you the maker. But even if they can't, *I know* and that's what's important." She smiled at him, "And didn't some handsome, young stud comment about how he liked the way I looked? Now that you have me on the defensive about *my* clothes, I must say I like your jeans. I like the way they fit most of all." She gave him a long, seductive kiss.

"Enough of that," he laughed.

Jana's face lit up as well and the seductive smile was his undoing. "There can never be enough as far as I'm concerned, but I can behave—if I have to."

The drive to the airport was relaxing but uneventful, in spite of Jana's teasing. Mike held her hand, more as protection to keep it away from his male parts, than out of a need for intimacy. He wanted her, but he wanted to wait until they were in Vegas.

As the car approached the departure gate Mike noticed a young lady out the window of the car. He closed his eyes and stifled a groan; maybe if they slowed down he would miss talking to her. Unfortunately he wasn't that lucky. If anything, Steven was very good at his job. The car stopped, and even though Mike waited for Steven to open the door for them, it wasn't long enough. Monique saw him and immediately rushed over. "Mike! It's so good to see you, how have you been, it has been ages," she leaned close and whispered, "I've missed you."

Mike forced a weak smile and reached back into the car to assist Jana with her exit.

Monique stepped back and gave Jana the once over.

"Mike, please introduce me to your friend," Jana whispered, staking her territory by placing her arm around his waist and letting her hand slide down and grab his buttocks.

"Jana, I want to introduce you to a friend from my college days, Monique; Monique, this is Jana a-friend-from work."

"Nice to meet you," Jana said, extending her hand.

"Nice to meet you too," Monique ignored the outstretched hand. "Mike, I thought we were more than *friends.*" Monique turned to Mike, putting her back to Jana and planting herself between the couple. "So, Mike, when are we going to get together again, I've been hesitant to call you, I was hoping you would make the first move. The argument we had was so silly and I really do want to see you again."

Mike couldn't believe Monique's rudeness. He reached behind her and took Jana's hand, pulling her toward him and placing his hand around her waist. "Monique, there's no *us*, I've moved on. I'm sorry; we need to catch our flight. It was good to see you, take care of yourself."

Jana saw Steven place the suitcases on the ground and make ready to resolve a difficult situation if needed. She gave him a subtle 'not yet' gesture with her eyes and he relaxed by the car. Steven was more than a driver, often accompanying her and other executives on trips as a driver and security escort.

Monique stood, hands on hips, and yelled, "So you're leaving me for someone old enough to be your mother?"

"Actually," Mike calmly replied, "leaving is not the right word, it's *left* you. Have a nice life." He escorted Jana into the terminal.

"That was fun," Jana whispered, rising on her toes to give him a kiss on the cheek. "Thanks for being my knight in shining armor."

"I'm sorry. When I saw her I knew she'd make a scene. That's always been her forte. She has to be the center of attention, and she can't stand to be upstaged by anyone. Hopefully she isn't going to Vegas too," he laughed.

"Wouldn't that be unfortunate," Jana shuddered.

*****

The Venetian hotel took Mike's breath away. His head turned left and right, up and down, craning to take in every fresco and gold gilded carving. He had never been in such luxury. The artwork, the rooms, everything was spectacular. "Not sure I've brought the right clothes for this place," he mumbled as he unpacked and hung his suit in the closet.

"There are no right clothes for Las Vegas. Watch the people and you'll agree. They come in all shapes and sizes and every costume available. Some dress up and some don't, and no one cares. That's what makes this place so much fun." She finished her own packing, "Okay, now what do you want to do? We have three hours until the show. We can go play tourist or we can just stay here and enjoy the luxury of the room. The bathtub looks inviting as well, but I'm open to anything."

"I'd like to just relax here for a while if you don't mind. This is a nice room it'd be a shame not to enjoy all the amenities. I'd like to order a snack from room service since dinner won't be until later this evening, would you like something too?"

"Actually yes, have them send up a pitcher of iced tea with lots of Sweet and Low. I'd also like a small Caesar salad. That should hold me over until dinner."

"Good idea, think I'll get a turkey club, you can help me eat it and maybe you'll let me share part of your salad."

"Sure that works for me."

Mike called room service, "They said it would be here in thirty minutes." He began to walk around the room like a caged animal, surveying his surrounding, looking for each and every escape route. He could feel Jana watching his every move. He turned on the flat screen television, getting acquainted with the remote, then turned it off. Another remote sat on the table and Mike picked it up to see what it did too. Playing with this remote control he realized it opened and closed the curtains. "Wow, that's pretty fancy." He walked into the bathroom, and saw another flat screen television in the corner. "This is so cool; I can watch ESPN and take a bath at the same time."

Jana walked in behind him, placing her arms around his waist, pressing her breasts into his back. "We don't do television in the bathroom young man."

"We don't?" Turning, he took her into his arms.

"No, bathrooms are for cleaning one's self and unadulterated sex, nothing else."

"Well the first concept I'm fully aware of," his hands slipped under her jacket, "but the last you're going to have to show me, as I've never experienced that side of a bathroom's utility." Just as his hand reached her breast there was a knock at the door. "Damn! What timing," he grunted as he walked to the door.

*****

"I enjoyed that, even though I think you ate more of my salad than I did, but I forgive you, as I think I got the better part of your sandwich." Jana groaned and rubbed her stomach to assist with the digestion, "I ate too much."

"I would say that makes us even," Mike said. "Now back to that bathroom utility thing you spoke of earlier. Would you like me to run you a bath, one we could share? We could watch the ball game at the same time," he laughed.

"I'll agree with part 'a', but part 'b' is out…no ball game. You're going to be too busy to watch sports. Besides, I don't want you distracted while I'm explaining the purpose of a bathroom."

"I'll go start the water," Mike got up and began taking off his clothes. By the time he reached the bathroom door he was fully aroused and beautifully naked.

Jana laughed, *such an eager young man.* She heard him turn on the water, "Not too hot, okay," she yelled. She removed her jacket and pants and walked into the bathroom wearing only a burnt orange lace bra and panties. She stepped to him and wrapped her arms around his neck. "Did you hear me about the water temperature?"

"Yes ma'am, I took care of it." Mike unfastened her bra, kissing her shoulders as he removed it, the wispy lace falling away to reveal her full breasts. He dropped to his knees and slowly pulled off her panties, holding them to his face and inhaling her scent. "Do you want me to get in first?"

"Yes," she smiled and tousled the hair of her kneeling lover, "I think that would be best."

Mike lowered himself in the tub and held out his hand to assist Jana with her entry.

She turned her back to him as she entered the water, and lowered herself to sit in front of him. She leaned back and relaxed in the warm scented water. "They had bath salts in here too?"

"These guys think of everything. Can I turn on the television now?" he smirked.

"No, you can't turn on the television." She took his hands and placed one on each breast. "Use these as your remote control; see what you can turn on by fiddling with *these*."

"I'm not sure of the channel selection but I'll see what's available." Mike turned her to face him and eased his erection into her, feeling the warmth of her tightly wrap around him. He began to lift his hips slowly, pumping in and out, enjoying every second of pleasure, but Jana indicated a need for more. Immediately he sped up his rhythm. Soon her moans and gasps changed to short, deep groans, and he knew she was about to climax. He continued his rapid, steady pace, and within seconds she put her hands on the side of the tub and cried out that she was coming. Her fingers found his shoulders and dug deeply into the skin, her moans loud and irregular. Mike knew she was on the edge and he pushed harder to help heighten her explosion. Suddenly he felt her tighten around him, and she came with so much force it was all he could do to stay inside her. Water was everywhere; in fact, there was more on the floor than in the tub.

Jana collapsed into Mike's arms. "I sure hope the floor is waterproof, or the folks below us aren't going to be too happy." She smiled and purred, "That was amazing. Can we do it again?"

Mike had yet to orgasm, and he was positive the answer to her question was *yes*, but he wanted to continue their sexual escapade in that beautiful king size bed. "Let's get out of here, and I'll see what I can do to accommodate your request."

Jana leaped to her feet, even though her knees were weak from the sexual experience they had already shared. She reached for a towel, wrapping her torso and watching Mike extract himself from the tub. *What a gorgeous hunk of man flesh you are little boy.* She handed him a towel and shook out her hair. "I'm going to have to take a shower and do my hair before we go tonight. It'll take me a good hour to put all the pieces together so we need to plan accordingly."

"Then we've no time to waste with useless chatter." He lifted her into his arms and walked to the bed. The bed was already turned down and the pillows propped alluringly for sex. *The little minx, she expected this.* Within seconds he positioned himself with her on top, and his cock buried inside her again.

She raised her head, shook back her hair and leaned down to suck his nipples, first one then the other. Jana placed her hands on his chest and began to rub his nipples between her fingers. She rubbed his nipples harder, "I want to feel your orgasm."

His heart was pounding and yet he held back, wanting to enjoy the moment as long as possible.

"Wait," Jana whispered. "Don't come yet. I want to make you come in a very special way."

He stopped, exerting all his control to remain still and let her take control. He felt a pulling sensation, as she began to contract and relax her female muscles. Within seconds his orgasm peaked and he exploded into her. Mike pulled her to him and she melted into his arms. "That was unbelievable. You're utterly amazing. What exactly was that anyway?"

"Men often forget the capacity a woman has to control the muscles of her body." She tenderly kissed his forehead. "I wanted you to experience what I can do for you as much as I appreciate what you do for me." The satiated feline predator laid her head on his shoulder, closing her green eyes.

Mike felt her breathing slow. He reached around her, setting his watch for thirty minutes. Blissfully he joined her in sleep, cuddling even closer with each breath. When his alarm went off, he was surprised to find Jana gone. He heard the shower, smiled, and walked in the bathroom, carrying with him a full erection and some great expectations.

Jana saw him and laughed, holding the shower door closed. "No—no you don't, we won't make the show if I let you in here in that condition. I'm almost done so you can have the shower shortly. Go away," she teased.

"You don't know what you're missing," he posed, shamelessly exposing himself, "but I can wait." As if on cue, his erection subsided as he approached the sink to shave.

Jana exited the shower and stood next to him, totally naked as they completed their individual toiletries. Mike stepped into the shower as Jana sat at the dressing table to finish putting on her makeup. It was hard to concentrate with a view of Mike's naked body visible in the vanity mirror. *I need to concentrate, or I'm going to have eye shadow on my lips and lipstick on my cheek. Damn, he's nice to look at. Real man candy.* Sighing, she left to dress.

Mike walked out of the bathroom and couldn't believe his eyes. Jana stood in front of him putting on her earrings, in a black backless evening dress. "Wow, you're absolutely stunning."

"Thanks, now hurry and get dressed or we'll be late." She brushed her lips across his and instantly followed with her thumb to wipe the lipstick from his lips.

"What are you wearing?"

"It's a Roberto Cavali, do you like it?"

"Yea! It's hot. I like the fact that your back is so exposed and the way it fits you."

"Its crepe," she beamed, knowing he didn't know what that meant.

"I'm somewhat familiar with different fabrics. My mom does a lot of sewing. When I was little she used to take me with her to classes. I had to sit in the corner and be good, but I listened and really learned quite a bit. She made costumes for us at Halloween and made dresses for my sister all the time. Now she mostly quilts." He ran his hand along her hip, feeling the fabric. "No, I don't think I've ever felt this type of fabric before. How do you expect me to keep my hands to myself knowing how great this feels?"

"You can touch as much as you want for the next three or four hours, you just can't take it off. Now get dressed we have a reservation in twenty minutes."

"Yes ma'am, I'll be ready in a minute."

Jana waited patiently, watching him get ready. It didn't take long and he was ready: dark suit, white shirt and silk tie. *What a gorgeous hunk of man candy, all mine; better than Jelly Bellies and not fattening.*

*****

Jana and Mike stood in line for the Phantom Theatre. "Let me give you a little background, so you know what to expect." Jana said.

"The theatre was designed by David Rockwell, a most talented designer. It recreates an old opera house setting; gives it a real *Phantom* feel. You'll love it. We have great seats in the center of the theater. When we get inside will you go to the top of the stairs and get me some water?"

"I feel like a little kid. This is so exciting; sure I'll get water for you. Have you seen this before?" His eyes were everywhere, taking in every nuance of his surroundings.

"Yes, I came when it first started showing and I've always wanted to come back."

Mike noticed a distinguished looking woman standing to their left. "Jana, is that woman trying to get your attention?"

"Who?" Looking around Jana spotted Sami.

"Sami, how are you? It's so good to see you." The two women hugged each other. "What are you doing in the Venetian?" Jana rolled her eyes, "No, don't tell me, you aren't getting married again?"

Sami smiled a reluctant smile, "Yes, tomorrow evening, right here. Is that why you're here? Did Charlie tell you?"

"No to both questions, Charlie didn't say a word."

"I didn't tell him until this morning, but he should be on a flight now, and will be here late tonight. He said I change husbands like he changes socks, but I really hope he does that more frequently," Sami laughed, "Jana, you have to meet him, he's great." Sami found David and signaled him to come over. "Jana, let me introduce you to my soon-to-be husband, David. David, this is one of my dearest friends, Jana Gates."

"I'm pleased to meet you," David offered his hand. It's nice that some of Sami's friends are going to be at our wedding after all. You are planning to come, right?"

Jana saw Sami's pleading eyes, "Sure we're in town for the big event. Let me introduce my new best friend; Mike Knight this is Sami Brandon and her fiance, David."

"It's great to finally meet both of you," Mike hugged Sami

and shook David's hand, "Jana hasn't stopped talking about this wedding since we got on the plane this afternoon. We can't wait, and with Charlie coming in as well, it'll be great."

Sami thanked him, turning to David, and giving him a big hug. "See honey, my family cares and they'll be here.

Jana gave Sami a hug. "We're staying in the Venetian, give me a call tomorrow with the details so we can be there. You are a prize old woman; but he appears to love you."

"It was great meeting you Mike, and Jana I'll call you tomorrow; early I promise. I've got a business meeting in the afternoon with a new accounting firm I'm looking to hire, but I'll call before I leave for that meeting. We're off for dinner with David's brother and his mom. Talk to you soon."

Mike furrowed his eyebrows, "Jana, what was her name?"

"Sami Brandon, why?"

"Does she normally go by Sam Brandon?"

"Yes, for her business, as she's found most men don't want to talk to a woman, but after they take her first call it usually isn't a problem. In the construction business Sami finds it's still very much a man's world. Why do you ask?" Mike was white as a sheet, "Are you okay?"

"*I'm* the new owner of the accounting firm she's meeting with tomorrow. Oh, this is awful. Now I feel like I'm meeting her under false pretenses. I don't want this job because she knows you; maybe I should cancel the meeting?"

"What kind of money does her hiring your firm represent?"

"Jeez, I would say it could be anywhere from a $100K to $500K retainer with the need for accountants on the staff full time. She's got a huge conglomerate if my numbers are even close. I've done a workup of her company structure and it's a major player in the Nevada and Arizona area. It would be a great coup to get her account first time out. But I can't meet with her now. Now that she knows I'm with one of her friends."

Jana couldn't slap him, not in public, so she grabbed his

hand and squeezed, "Calm down! You may know a lot about her business, but you know nothing about the woman. Let me give you some insight. First of all, Sami wouldn't care if you were my first born and in desperate need of work. If she knew you couldn't do the job she wouldn't hire you. You'll find that tomorrow she'll act like she doesn't know you, and by the time your meeting is over you won't be sure you ever met her before. Business and pleasure don't mix for her. She works hard and she plays hard, but she never, and I mean never, mixes the two. So, you go to the meeting tomorrow and you do your thing, and if you get her account it'll be because you sold it, not because you're my Las Vegas boy-toy."

"But Charlie's her son, and he works with me. I'm sleeping with one of her best friends. I can't believe that won't matter to her." His lips split into a wide grin, "I'm your boy-toy?"

She pinched his cheek, "Focus, boy-toy. She'll care that you know her son and that the two of you are friends, as she cares who I see and that I'm happy, but like I said, she doesn't mix business and pleasure. Just wait and see. Oh good, they're opening the doors. Let's put this aside for now and enjoy our evening, please." She pushed him toward the door. "Our seats are down, two rows in the middle. I'll sit down and you go and get the water, okay?"

"Sure, be right back, save me a seat." He walked to the back of the theater, contemplating what had just transpired. *What have I done? I might have blown the entire reason I made this trip. If Jana's right, and Ms Brandon doesn't mix work with pleasure, it'll be fine. I can't pass up this opportunity. Damn, my uncle is going to kill me.* He bought two bottles of water and walked hesitantly to their seats.

I have to take his mind off this meeting with Sami or it will spoil our whole evening. As Mike joined Jana he handed her the water. She grabbed his tie and pulled him in for a kiss that rolled down his socks.

"Wow, what was that for?" he whispered.

"I just wanted you to think about what was to come," she brushed her hand along the front of his pants.

"Stop that, this is no time for games." He looked around making sure no one noticed.

"This is *not* a game, I'm dead serious. I figure we have a little over ninety minutes in the dark of this theater where we can enjoy the show, or we can enjoy the show and a little of each other."

"Jana, there are people all around us, surely you aren't suggesting...?"

"Mike, put your arm around me and slide your hand down around my waist."

Mike realized with just the slightest move of his hand he could hold her right breast, doing so he felt her nipple respond to his touch.

She whispered, "Now turn yourself more toward me and move your suit coat over the front of you pants." He shifted in his seat. "No a little more, now reach down and unzip your suit pants."

"Jana, I'm going to get arrested for indecent exposure if this continues." Even so he did exactly as she instructed.

"No, you aren't, we aren't taking things out for show and tell, we're just making them accessible to an interested hand." As the lights dimmed Jana reached over and laid her hand on his thigh allowing easy access. "Now, sit back my love and enjoy the show."

He enjoyed one of the best productions in history, and his date; he had a very desirable, very beautiful woman's right breast in his hand and he knew from her nipple that she was excited. The feeling was reciprocated as Jana began to caress his erection through his pants.

Jana asked, "Are you thinking about Sami?"

"Hell no, have you lost your mind, I can't think at all." He brought his hand to her shoulder and held her close.

Jana, without pause, zipped his pants and placed her hand on his leg. His mind was now where she wanted it.

*****

At the Delmonico Steakhouse Mike informed the hostess of their reservations and was told it would be a few minutes. He escorted Jana to the bar and ordered her a Pomegranate martini and himself a Guinness. They had barely received their drinks when the hostess came to escort them into dinner. As the waiter advised them of the specials Mike knew what she wanted without even asking. He thanked the young man and ordered without asking her. "Yes the lady and I will both have filet mignon steak medium, twice baked potatoes and we'll split a side of asparagus. We'll each have a bowl of your New Orleans Gumbo and two iced teas with dinner and sparkling water." The waiter wrote it all down, nodded and walked away.

"I think I should be mad at you," Jana whispered.

"Why? Isn't that what you wanted?"

"Well yes, but you didn't even ask me. I'm glad I didn't have to correct you on anything, but in the future, for your own safety, even though you're sure you're right, ask me."

"I'm sorry, I'm glad I got it right, and in the future I'll ask. Tell you what."

"What?"

"You can pick dessert." The Gumbo arrived, "This is fantastic. I don't think I've ever eaten anything with such flavor. Usually I don't like Gumbo."

"Really?" Jana cocked her head, "Why'd you order it then?"

"Because Charlie said it was one of your favorites and I figured if you liked it I needed to give it a try. You're right, as usual, it's great."

Jana laughed. "So I can thank Charlie for the knowledge of my eating habits."

"Yes and no. I'm glad you like steak, as it's my favorite in almost any form. Of course I've never had one here, but if the soup is any indication of your taste I know I'm in for a treat.

"You are priceless. What would you have done if you didn't like what you ordered? What if I was a vegetarian?"

"I'd have eaten my vegetables and told you how good it was, and then order a hamburger from room service while you were sleeping," he laughed.

"Don't do that anymore okay? Order what you want and I'll order what I want. If you want to try something I order then I'll give you a taste, and if you like it the next time you can order it. It'll also give me an opportunity to try some of the things you like as well, agreed?"

"Agreed," he smiled. Looking pensive, he asked, "Jana, you're a fantastic lady, and I know this is none of my business, but if you wouldn't mind, I'd like to know. What happened to you and Craig? How does a marriage of over twenty years just end?"

Jana spooned asparagus onto her plate. "Are you sure you want to hear this? It's not that exciting, in fact it's pretty poor dinner conversation."

"I'd like to understand it, and make sure I don't make the same mistake."

"Okay, I'll give you the short version. You know we were married young, I turned twenty one a few days after we were married in fact. We grew up together and were together in our last years of high school. I have a daughter about your age, just in case you didn't know." She shuddered at that thought. "She's married now, and left home when she was in her late teens. Craig and I worked together the last ten years of our lives enjoying our successes and failures together. In the last couple of years we grew apart. I was traveling to one place and him to another and we just didn't seem to take the time to be with each other."

"I know this is hard for you, but what caused the break up?"

"You're going to think I'm silly and petty, but here goes. There was an award banquet where Craig was getting recognized for one thing or another, I can't even remember what. Isn't that sad? Anyway he stood up and thanked everyone there who had helped him achieve his success, everyone but me and I was right by his side. In fact I helped plan the event. When it was over I left the event with him, expecting him to say something and he didn't. When we got home I asked him if he realized he thanked almost everyone in the room but me. Funny thing was he didn't realize it. He apologized and at the time I was fine with it, but I wasn't. I was hurt. It kept me awake all night and the next day, I packed my bags and walked away. He was there and it didn't take him long to realize what I was doing, but he made no attempt to stop me. Later we tried to talk about it and finally we agreed this was best for both of us. Yes, there were rumors of other women he'd been with during our marriage, and true or not, I didn't believe them. We'd made a promise to each other when we married that if we ever wanted to be with someone else we'd get a divorce first. Since he never asked for a divorce I figured he hadn't found anyone else. I've always believed for a marriage to work you have to work at it 24/7. I guess we just stopped putting that kind of effort into it. That's the short version."

"One more question and then I'll stop, do you ever intend to marry again?"

"I really don't know. I'd have to say yes, but not right now. Even though our divorce was amiable, it was very hard. I lost my best friend and confident, and I'm not ready to take that kind of chance again, at least not in the immediate future. Enough about me, what about you, do you want to be married, have a family?"

"Sure, someday, I guess haven't thought much about it."

"That's because you haven't met the right person yet, but I'm confident you will, and when that happens they'll be no stopping you. Did you enjoy your steak?"

"Yes, excellent choice if I must say so myself," he laughed. "I'm not sure whether to thank you or Charlie."

"Very funny! Tell you what, let's get out of here. I want to lose some money in the slot machines and then I know this very eligible young man who promised me a night to remember."

Mike signaled the waiter for the check. He escorted Jana back to the casino floor, "I'll let you play for a while. I'm not much of a gambler so I'll walk around and check out the sights. Don't worry about moving around; I'll find you." He kissed her, deeply, with more passion than he ever had before and then turned and walked through the casino.

*****

Jana picked up her ringing cell phone, "Hello."

"Where are you?" Mike hollered over the noise of the casino.

"I'm in the room, waiting for this young stud muffin who promised to find me in the casino, but when he never showed I came up to the room hoping he would be here."

"Sorry, jeez, I met a friend at the bar and lost track of time. I'm on my way up; do you want me to bring anything?"

"Yes, a cold bottle of water if you don't mind."

"I'm on my way." Mike stopped cold when he opened the door to the room; there was a rose petal path leading to the bed. Faux electric candles were lit all around the room. Jana lounged on the bed, surrounded by pillows. She wore only a satin and lace mauve nightgown, the sides split to the waist, and the neckline meeting the waist band in the front. Delicate ties at the shoulders were all that kept it on. "Do... Do you want this—water. Now?"

"No, it can wait." She curled her finger and beckoned him forward. "What I want right now is you, naked," she purred.

Mike didn't wait to be asked twice. Within seconds he was climbing the bed from the bottom up, slowly trying to determine exactly where she wanted him. He kissed her toes, sucking each one as he massaged one foot and then the other. Jana's moans confirmed she enjoyed his foot worship. He continued to take little nips and placed kisses along her legs and up her thighs. Mike moved up her entire body spreading her legs with his knees. He kissed each breast, taking the nipple through the fabric, and using his teeth to pull it toward him. Every touch was sensual as he moved further up her body, nipping at her neck and finally reaching her mouth. He made love to her mouth, using his tongue to attack hers. They couldn't get enough of each other. Mike eased the pillows out from behind her, laying her down on the bed as he entered her slowly. He paused every few seconds, and though he could tell by her movements she wanted him, he made her wait. Fully plunging into her, he felt her gasp and then relax, letting him fill her. He pulled almost completely out of her, held for a second and then entered her again, stronger, deeper.

Jana moved from side to side trying to meet his movements, trying to get him to make love to her and not torture her, but she couldn't get his attention. She moved her hands to his chest rubbing his nipples and twisting them with her fingers. This didn't stop his teasing, it only intensified his moves. In, almost out, back in. God, it was pure torture, of the most exquisite kind. Slowly her energy built as her orgasm surfaced. It shattered her, making her cry out in pure joy.

Mike waited while Jana gained control. He was hard again, and ready for another round. He rolled her over on top and she took charge, riding him like a rodeo star. She flexed her muscles, not allowing him to move unless she did. She was definitely in control, moving forward and back, rotating her hips and allowing him to fondle her breasts. He untied the gown and let the top fall open. He greedily took one and then the other of her breasts into his mouth while she rode him hard.

Jana felt him begin to shudder, so she slowed and encouraged his attention to her breasts. He was confused and didn't know exactly what to do, but his hips never stopped moving as she bucked up and down, round and round. Jana felt him shudder as she climaxed, but he never missed a beat. His attention to her breasts never faltered, even when he allowed her to move off him. His hand moved between her legs and he stroked the same area his cock had just vacated. She squirmed against his hand, riding it in a similar fashion while he continued to lick and suck at her breasts. Moaning, she climaxed once again and Mike felt the contractions against his fingers. He pulled her close, holding her in his arms.

"Sleep now," she whispered.

"Sleep now, indeed," he replied as he reached down and pulled up the covers. "Jana, are you asleep?" he whispered.

She didn't answer, but snuggled closer into his arms as she eased into sleep.

"Marry me, Jana," Mike whispered.

She heard him, but she couldn't answer. She couldn't make herself answer; instead she closed her eyes and bit her lip, a tear falling down her check.

Mike waited for an answer, received none, and assumed she was asleep. He'd ask her tomorrow and he nodded off beside her.

Jana lay awake in his arms for an hour without moving. She didn't want to get married, but she didn't want to hurt Mike. She needed to be honest and upfront with him if he asked again. Hopefully it was lust, the heat of the moment and he really didn't mean it. Hopefully.

Nine

Jana woke to the sound of running water, and looked over to see what time it was. She had to get up, she had no choice. *I've got to go to the bathroom.* Still groggy, she walked into the bathroom. Mike was singing in the shower.

"Good morning beautiful."

Jana moaned, "Yea, good morning. What are you so cheerful about?"

"It's a beautiful day, and once I get done with my meeting we have the rest of the weekend together." He stepped from the shower and wrapped a towel around his waist. He reached for Jana, pulling her toward him for a kiss.

"You're getting me all wet," she laughed as she wiggled away. "I'm going back to bed. *You* have meetings, but I don't have any plans. Sam couldn't get me a spa treatment, so all I've got to do today is find a dress for Sami's wedding. Do you need me to get you anything?"

"Could you see if the hotel can have my shirt laundered and my suit pressed? I was in such a hurry last night; I didn't hang them up when I took them off."

"I'm sure they can handle it. I'll call you after I hear from Sami about what time the wedding is. I'll leave a message on your phone. You said before you thought you would be back by four so that should work fine. I'd like to do an early dinner, and then we can see where we go after the wedding."

He kissed her good-bye, "That's fine with me. I'm out of here. Enjoy your day. I don't need to worry about you do I?"

"No, I'm capable of entertaining myself. Granted it's not as good without you, but I'll manage," she put her hand over her eyes in mock drama, "Good luck with your meeting. I can't wait to hear how it goes. Hey, if I run into Charlie do you mind if I ask him to meet us for dinner?"

"No that's fine." She heard the door close behind him.

Sleep, I need more sleep, then shopping. She hugged the pillow to her chest and began to drift off to sleep. The ringing phone brought her straight up in bed. Grumbling, she answered, "What!"

"Jana, is that you?" Sami asked hesitantly.

"Yes, sorry, I was just getting back to sleep and the phone rang. What's up Sami?"

"The wedding is at seven on a bridge over the Grand Canal amid the sights and sounds of St. Mark's Square. It's called a Ponte al di Piazza, Bridge Over the Square, wedding. It was David's choice, as you must have guessed, because if I'd had my choice we'd have done one of those drive-thru jobs," Sami laughed. "Even Charlie thought it was appropriate, that way if he didn't want anyone to know he was part of the wedding party he could just walk off and no one would care. You don't think he'd do that, do you?"

"No, Sami he won't do that; Charlie loves you. Besides, he doesn't want you to disown him. Is he here; have you spoken to him?"

"Yes, he's here, I just woke him up with the same information. Maybe you two should get together as you're both grumpy this morning. What happened to your young man; did he leave you high and dry?"

"My young man is none of your business," Jana laughed. "Listen, I'll see you tonight. I think I'll call Charlie and see if he wants to hang out with me today since my young man has plans. See you later Sami." Jana called the front desk, asked for Charles Brandon's room, and the phone rang.

"Mom, you'd better be dead," Charlie grumbled.

"First of all it isn't mom, and no, I'm not dead."

"Jana, sorry, what's the problem?"

"There's no problem. I just got off the phone with your mom and she said she had awakened you too, so I figured I'd see if you wanted to join me for breakfast."

"Doable, but it'll take me an hour to get ready and I need to get the hotel to press my suit for tonight."

"I'll meet you at Bouchon's in an hour. Depending on the time we can have breakfast or lunch."

"Works for me, hey wait a minute. You want something, don't you? I know you, you need someone to shop with you; is that why you're asking me to meet you?"

"See you in an hour Charlie, don't be late." She hung up.

Jana arrived before Charlie and asked the hostess to seat her so she could get some much needed coffee. She definitely needed the caffeine this morning. As the waiter poured her coffee, she watched Charlie enter.

He gave her a quick kiss on the cheek. "You look well. It's obvious this weekend agrees with you and it hasn't even been a full twenty four hours."

"Yes it does, and don't be an ass Charlie. It was a surprise to see your mom last night. You didn't say anything about her getting married again."

"Hell, I didn't know until after you left yesterday. I left a message on your cell phone, didn't you get it?"

"No, sorry, I didn't notice. Well, anyway, glad you're here and I know your mom is glad too."

"She's so cute," Charlie said. "She's afraid I won't like him. What kind of young man marries a woman old enough to be their mother anyway? I told her it wasn't a concern whether I liked him or not. Question is, does she like him? She says she loves him, and she knows he'll make her happy. That's really all I want as well. I don't need a new father; I just want my mom happy. She works too hard and she definitely needs someone to grab her attention once in a while so she slows down. What did you think of him?"

"He's very handsome and obviously loves her very much. He was really happy to think Mike and I had come here for the wedding and to learn that you were flying in as well." Jana nodded to the waiter when he asked if she'd like more coffee. "I take it your mom wasn't really intending to invite anyone?"

"That's what she told me this morning. She said David wanted his family there. I guess his brother and his wife and his mom are here. Did you meet them too?" Charlie took a piece of the bread, added a large dab of butter and jam, and placed it in his mouth, savoring the taste.

"No, they weren't with them. If I remember right they were going to meet them at the same time Mike and I were going into the Phantom, which by the way was great."

"So where's Mike?" Charlie mumbled through a mouthful of bread.

"You aren't going to believe this one. Mike's in a meeting with your mom. It seems Brandon, Inc. is looking for a new accounting firm to take on their business and she is interviewing Mike's new company for the job. Mike was a nervous wreck when he put the pieces together last night, and it took me a while to convince him that your mom didn't mix her personal life with her business. I also told him your mom didn't do favors, nor hire people because of who they knew, I'm right aren't I?"

"Pretty much, unless Mike can hold his own he won't get the job. This is going to be fun. You know mom won't make a decision on the spot, I mean she'll have decided, but if Mike gets the job she's going to make him wait for an answer. Is Mike planning to be your escort for the wedding?" Charlie grabbed the last piece of bread before Jana had a chance.

"Sure, Sami invited us both. She knew Mike was with me. But I have a favor to ask you, and it's not just giving me part of that," She pointed to the bread on Charlie's plate.

"I knew it. You want me to take you shopping."

"Yes, but only to the Fashion Show Mall. I just need to go to Nordstrom's. I called them before I came down and they have this gorgeous Dolce & Gabbana stretch satin bustier dress with exposed boning that would be just right for your mom's wedding. I have an appointment in one hour to get a fitting, and they guarantee me they can have it ready within an hour, so we need to eat and get moving."

Charlie ate the bread, ignoring her request. "What else do you have to get, there's always more." He grinned, "I didn't share this with you because I want to make sure you can fit into that dress."

"You're a rat." She smacked him on the shoulder. "As for what else I need, I'd like to get a shirt for Mike and a tie and pocket hanky that will match my dress." Watching Charlie grimace she continued, "Come on, it'll be fun and you can get a new shirt and tie too. You like to shop almost as much as I do, admit it."

"No one likes to shop as much as you do, but I could use a new shirt and tie and a pair of shoes. If you'll help me pick them out then I'll be your escort to the mall. I can't believe I'm doing this."

"Quit whining, you know you love to go shopping with me. We have the best time when we do this. People always think you're my son. I think I'll look at shoes too as I doubt if anything I brought will match that dress."

"Where's a gun when you need it," he laughed as he looked over the menu.

Jana finished her Croque Madame and Charlie his Salmon Baguette, and they sat back and enjoyed the delicious coffee. "Charlie, I'm worried about this Cougar thing."

He saw the confusion on her face, "What do you mean-worried?"

"I mean, is this a smart thing to do? Here I am in a hotel with a man young enough to be my son. I'm not sure if I was the mother of that son, I'd be really happy with the circumstances of this relationship."

"I guess that could be a concern, but Jana you need to quit putting your mid-west morality into this equation. Today is different than yesterday, and all you're really doing is what men have been doing for centuries. How many men do you know who have left their wives for a young secretary, or had an affair with a younger woman?"

Jana reluctantly nodded, conceding Charlie's point, "I know what you're saying is true, but it doesn't help me rationalize this in my public mind. In the privacy of our room this is fun, exciting," she sighed, "and exhausting. But when we walk through the casino I notice folks looking at us, wondering what the old lady is doing with the younger man. I guess it's just more accepted for men to do than women."

"Again a true statement," Charlie said, "but the barriers for this type of relationship are coming down all around us. As women become more dominant, more aware of their own worth and ability to make their own decisions, they are enjoying these type of relationships as much as men do. I have a recommendation for you, are you listening?"

"Sure, I'm listening."

"Jana, enjoy your time with Mike. Enjoy the friendship, enjoy the sex, and when you two go your separate ways, say thanks for all that you've been able to give to each other."

"I'll try, hell I *am* trying, but it's hard to have this type of physical relationship without the emotional involvement."

"You're not wired to just have casual sex. Whether you want to believe it or not, there is an emotional tie to Mike. But are you in love with him Jana? Is that what you're saying here?" Charlie's concern was evident on his face.

"No, I'm not in love, if anything I'm in perpetual lust. Is that wrong?"

"No, it's not wrong, just take it a day at a time and enjoy your time with Mike. There are no rules that say you can't have sex with any man, or woman for that matter, who is a consenting adult. I'm pretty sure Mike fits into that equation and I can't see why you wouldn't want to be with him as time permits."

"Okay, thanks Charlie, I think I've got a handle on it. How on earth did you get so wise for someone so young?"

"God, you're making me crazy. I think you need retail therapy. Let's go shopping."

*****

Charlie and Jana enjoyed the Venetian limo ride to the mall.

Charlie whispered, "Jana we could have taken a taxi."

"Why would we do that when this limo was sitting there doing nothing? He's ours for the afternoon, so we can go anywhere we want."

"I only want to go to the mall and then back to the hotel. I'd really like to get a nap in before the wedding if possible."

"Mike was going to meet me for an early dinner, you want to join us?"

"No, I'll pass. Think I'll order a hamburger and a couple of beers from room service. There's a ball game on later this afternoon I'd like to catch."

In Nordstrom's Jana went to women's formal wear and asked for Nora, who appeared within seconds with the dress, a pair of matching shoes, and clutch in hand. "I didn't know exactly what you'd need, so I came prepared," Nora said breathlessly.

"This is fantastic, let me try them on and we can see where we go from here. What do you think Charlie?"

"It's an exquisite dress. I hope the bride is as beautiful or you're going to be the center of attention."

"Really, is it too much you think?"

"It's beautiful, go try it on. I'll take a seat over there and wait for the fashion show."

"Your mother's very beautiful," Nora said.

"Yes, she is, very beautiful," Charlie said, his thoughts focused on his mom and the wedding. *I hope you know what you're doing mom. I really want you to be happy.*

Jana walked from the fitting room, and shifted back and forth in front of the mirror taking it all in. "Well, what do you think?"

"It's like it was made for you," Nora responded.

"She's right; it's perfect," Charlie said. "It fits well in all the right places, and I love the boning on both the front and back. The color is nice; it's a beautiful shade of Camel. The shoes work well with it too; a great selection Nora."

Nora blushed from ear to ear, "Thank you sir, just doing my job."

"Nora, Charlie's right they're perfect, both the dress and the shoes, and I'll take the matching clutch as well. Now we need some men's items, can you help us with them as well?"

"Yes, I can, what exactly are you looking for?"

"We need a couple of shirts, one that matches this dress with a tie and hanky to go with it. Then we need a shirt for Charlie here, and a tie and hanky as well, and he also needs a pair of dress shoes."

"I will meet you down in men's apparel. I want to put your dress into a carry bag and get your shoes and purse bagged as well. It'll take me about ten minutes."

"Not a problem, we'll meet you in the men's shoe department." Charlie took Jana's hand and led her to the escalator. "That wasn't too bad at all. You bought a dress, shoes and a purse in less than twenty minutes. That's got to be a first," he laughed.

Jana laughed too. "You are so cute. Let's see if you can pick out shoes, a shirt and tie with that same time line."

The limo took them back to the Venetian. Jana hoped Mike would like the items she bought for him.

The driver walked around and let them out. "Thanks for everything," Charlie said as he dropped a tip in his hand.

"You know, Charlie, you have the right idea. I think I'm going up and take a nap too." Shopping bags in hand, she walked to the elevator. "See you at the wedding."

Jana's head barely hit the pillow when she heard the door open.

Mike quietly entered the room, not knowing if she was there or not, and if she was there whether she was sleeping. They'd both been up quite late last night, and if there was a God he could use a nap as well. His meeting with Brandon hadn't gone bad, but he had no idea if his company was accepted or not. Sami Brandon gave nothing away; that was for sure.

As he walked into the room, Jana opened her eyes, "Did you just get back?"

"Yes, mind if I join you?"

"*Only* if you intend to sleep," she murmured into her pillow.

"Yes, I need a nap too."

"Okay then, you can join me," she pushed a pillow at him; "you stay on your side."

"Yes, ma'am!" Within minutes they were both asleep. Mike didn't know how it happened, but when he went to turn over he found Jana asleep in his arms. He cuddled into her and went back to sleep.

*****

With a nap behind them they both felt better. Jana ran a comb through her hair and decided it was fine for now. She would have to do it from scratch before the wedding but for now it would do. "Let's get some Mexican food."

"Sounds great, is there a place here?"

"Yes, there's a place downstairs, the Taqueria. It has a lot of the flavors of Old Mexico. If we get lucky we might be able to get seats along the Grand Canal. There's some terrific views of the Venetian streetscapes and the passing gondolas. They have things like Chile rellenos, tacos al carbon or shrimp quesadillas. You should be able to find something you like. Does that sound like it meets your needs?"

"It meets mine, what about yours?"

"Believe it or not it's one of my favorite places to eat, and I like the fact that it's casual dining. Besides that I love Mexican food and their Margaritas are great. Let's go." Hand in hand they left the room.

"Jana, did you get my suit taken care of for tonight?"

"Yes, it's hanging in the closet all ready to go."

"Great."

"How'd your meeting go?"

"Not sure. Ms Brandon, Sami, didn't make any decision today. I just have to be patient. It would be great for my company, but it's not a show stopper by any means. I'm just pleased she gave me a chance to compete."

As they approached the restaurant, Jana asked, "Well, what do you think?"

"Looks good, I'm starving." Mike asked the hostess for a table for two and along the water if available. She escorted them to a table.

A waiter quickly appeared to take their drink order. "I'd like a margarita please," Jana said.

"I'll take a Corona, thanks," Mike added, "Can we get chips and guacamole too?"

Jana narrowed her eyes, "Did Charlie tell you I liked guacamole too?"

"Actually no, I like it and I was hoping you did too." Mike smiled, "Did you see Charlie today?"

"Yes, he took me shopping. I asked him to join us for dinner, but he wanted to have a hamburger in his room and watch the ball game."

"Damn, there's a ball game on and here I sit. There are three, count them three, televisions in the room and I'm down here."

"You can go up any time you want." Jana blew him a kiss across the table. "I'll meet up with you later and you can tell me how the game ended."

Mike laughed, "No, I'm here with you. I'm sure Charlie will share the score with me later and I can always catch it when they rebroadcast it tonight if it was good. Truly," he smiled, "I want to stay here with you, really I do."

"Hmmm, I'm not sure I believe you, but I'm glad you're staying. You can catch the end of the game when we go up to the room. The wedding doesn't start until seven so we have lots of time once we're done here."

"Let's not talk about sports anymore. How was your shopping experience, where did you go? What did you buy?"

Jana leaned back dipped a chip in the salsa, "A sudden interest in fashion? Do you really care, or are you just making conversation?"

"I do care; and I truly want to know."

"We went to the Fashion Show Mall and I bought the prettiest camel colored Dolce & Gabbana stretch satin bustier dress with exposed boning. I picked up shoes and a clutch to match. You're going to love it."

"I'm not sure I know what all that means. Can you break it down for me? What exactly is a Dolce & Gabbana?"

She smiled, trying to figure out if he was pulling her leg. "They are two designers from Italy."

"And the bustier, boning thing?"

"I know you've seen women in a bustier, and I'm sure you've noticed the firm lines that surround it. In a quality bustier these firm lines are maintained with spiral steel, where in the early days they used whalebone, thus the term boning. Today they use mostly plastic, but in some garments they still use ivory, wood or cane as the stiffener. Most of the boning is under the surface of the garment. In the dress I bought today it's exposed, adding an accent to the dress." Under the table she ran the edge of her high heel along his leg and watched him shiver. "Exciting, yes?"

"I have this image in my mind. We'll just have to wait until you get dressed this evening to see how close my imagination comes to the real thing. Why'd Charlie go with you?"

"Actually his mom called and woke me up and told me she'd done the same to him a few minutes earlier. I called Charlie, woke him again, and invited him to breakfast. I sort of pressured him to go with me. He says he hates it, but he has good taste and I love going with him. Besides that he needed a couple of things too and I was more than happy to help."

"Let's go back to the room and relax before we have to go to the wedding. We have over an hour to get ready. Will it take you long?"

"Probably about an hour, I need to do my hair since I took a nap. I don't want to have bed hair at the wedding."

"You don't have bed hair," his eyes looked into hers, "you look great."

"I still want to shower and freshen up before we go. I know I'd feel better."

"Can I wash your back?" Mike asked, more of a plea than a question.

Jana shook her head, *the guy is relentless*. "Only if we hurry."

Mike signaled for the check, signing the bill. He took Jana's hand and they went to their room. Mike noticed the light flashing on the phone indicating there was a message. "Why don't you check that out while I go to the bathroom?"

Jana pressed the button and heard a message from Sami asking her to call her in Charlie's room. She dialed the room and waited.

Sami answered, "Yes, can I help you?"

"Sami, its Jana what's up?"

"Jana, good of you to call me back, is your young man there?"

"Yes, not exactly standing next to me, but in the room, why?"

"Well, I'm going to hire him, but I don't have time to talk right now. Do you want to tell him for me?"

"No, you do it tonight after the wedding, I'm sure you'll get a few minutes to speak to him."

"Thanks again for coming Jana; I know you weren't planning on it. Charlie said you made him take you shopping for a new dress."

"You know that boy of yours is lying through his teeth. He practically begged me to take him along." She laughed, "See you tonight, Sami."

As Mike entered the room he heard her last comment. "Was that Sami?"

"Yes, she was giving me a bad time about making Charlie go shopping with me today. I didn't force him, he wanted to go." She laughed as she began to unzip her cropped pants, wiggling them down her hips.

"Charlie's a big boy, if he didn't want to go I don't think you could have made him." Following suit Mike removed his clothes. They entered the shower and Jana turned on the water. Both of them were pressed against the walls waiting for the water to turn warm. Laughing, they came together under the warm spray.

Jana wet her hair and reached for the hair wash, her breasts sliding across Mike's skin.

"Can I help you with that?" Mike asked.

"No problem." Jana leaned back so Mike could wash her hair. He turned her slightly and gently pulled her head back as he rinsed the soap out. He took the cream rinse and applied it to her hair working it in as he'd seen her do earlier.

"Mmm," Jana moaned, "that's divine. Would you wash my back?"

"Sure!" Mike lathered up his hand and worked it slowly from her shoulders down her splendid tapered torso. She leaned slightly forward and tensed when his hands cupped her breasts. Mike knelt behind her and gently soaped her bottom, going down and up each leg. He turned her slowly and moved up her body washing every space he could, and some he probably didn't need to, but washed a second time just for fun. Mike questioned softly, "Is it my turn?"

Jana faced him, her eyes focused on his semi-rigid erection. "Definitely, I think you missed a spot, but I think I can fix that." She took the soap from his hand and knelt down. She slowly lathered his manhood and found there was nothing semi-rigid about it now. It had become an impressive cock. She finished washing his legs, turning him around to wash his back, "How's that?"

"You're a little tease, but you know that already. I think since you created this monster you need to enjoy what it has to offer."

"Well bring it on big boy! I've been waiting for you all day." She locked her arms around his neck and let Mike lift her off the floor while he separated her legs. She was primed and wet, and Mike slid into her easily. She reached around, locking her legs behind him, and began to move with him, intensifying the interaction.

Mike pushed her against the shower wall, taking her hands from around his neck and holding them against the wall, making her his prisoner of lust as he continued to make love to her.

Jana was consumed by the action. Mike's every movement increased the intensity ot their sexual coupling. She felt her release building and suddenly it swept through her, she convulsed in orgasmic release. Jana jerked her hands free and ran her fingers through Mike's hair.

Mike didn't want it to be over, and continued to plunge in and out of her.

Jana was tiring and leaned forward, pressing her breasts against Mike's chest. They kissed deeply, their tongues probing and twirling.

The pressure in Mike's loin was building again, and he knew Jana could feel it.

She sensed it, and began rotating her hips as he pumped up and down.

Mike exploded, grabbing her roughly, growling, his eyes shut tight and his toes curling. As he continued to drive into her, Jana came again, quivering and gasping. It was a long, satisfying orgasm for both of them. It took a minute for reality to return. Mike questioned softly, "Are you okay?"

"I'm better than okay," Jana gasped, "but I think I need another shower." She unhooked her legs and slid down Mike's muscled torso. "Tell you what, you stand in the corner and behave yourself while I get cleaned up. Then you can shower and we can get dressed for the wedding. Go on" she urged, "in the corner, hands behind your back."

Mike backed into the corner like a good little boy, and clasped his hands behind his back. Still, his biology betrayed him. Jana's domineering tone and her soapy, glistening naked body had his cock fully erect.

Jana turned, and her eyes grew wide at the sight of his erection. She reached out and slapped it, an act which made Mike wince, but not from pain. "THAT," Jana said, "is not going to come out and play now, maybe later." She smiled and winked at Mike as she left the shower, "Your turn."

Mike reached over and turned on more cold water. *I need to get control here, or I'm never going to be able to get dressed. I feel like I'm in constant heat around this woman. I can't remember when I've been so turned on.* Watching her towel off through the shower glass he turned the water to completely cold. As she walked from the room, Mike sighed as he finished showering. *What a woman!*

Jana was dressed when Mike walked from the bathroom. "Wow," Mike gave his best wolf-whistle, "that is *some* dress, and no it isn't what I pictured, it's better! I almost wish I'd been in Charlie's place today." Mike turned and rummaged in the closet for his shirt. "Did you send my white shirt out to be laundered?"

"No."

"No? Did you want me to go without a shirt?"

"No," she reached behind her and brought out the soft camel shirt with the tie and hanky, "I bought you one to match my dress."

"Jana, my white shirt would have been fine."

"I know, but I wanted us to be a couple tonight, and these types of things make me feel like we are, humor me, lover."

Smiling, he took the shirt and slipped it on. It was the softest thing he'd ever felt. "This is really nice, what's it made of?"

"Egyptian cotton."

"That explains it. It's very nice, thanks. It feels great against my skin and the tie is nice too." He saw exactly how the shirt and tie matched, and yet contrasted her dress. "You're right; we look like we planned to be at this wedding together. By the way I love your shoes, they're hot." He licked his lips, "You know, if we don't get out of here we aren't going to make this wedding; that I can guarantee you."

"Then let's go; I don't want to disappoint Sami or David."

Mike led the way to the door, but stopped short, turned and took Jana's hand in his. "I know you heard me last night when I asked you to marry me, didn't you?"

She bit her lip and looked away. *Shit! I was hoping this wouldn't come up.* "Yes, I heard you."

"Will you marry me, Jana?"

"No, Mike I won't. I love you, but not in that way. Wanting you physically is not enough to build a marriage on, though I know many couples who have tried. We've been together less than a week. That isn't enough time to really know each other." She saw him try to hide the pain of her words. "I know from that look that you don't agree. But please, on this one give me the benefit of the doubt. You're starting a new job here in a week. I live a four hour flight from here. This is not the basis of a good marriage. For now good friends is what we have to accept, and in the future, if this develops into more, we can take it from there. Please, this isn't a conversation for the hallways or elevator of this hotel. Can we please put this on hold until we get back to the room?"

"Yes, but the discussion's not over." He held her shoulders and looked into her eyes. "I don't disagree with you Jana, but I want to fully understand where we go from here before we leave this weekend."

"I agree, and we'll talk it through, all night if you want and all day tomorrow. But right now we have a wedding to enjoy." She closed her eyes knowing this wasn't going to be easy for either of them.

"Okay," Mike pulled her into his arms and kissed her.

When he broke the kiss Jana backed up and took a deep breath, "Stop that, or we aren't going to any wedding."

"If that's an alternative for the evening," Mike grinned, "all you have to do is give the word."

"You know we can't do that, now behave yourself." Jana pushed Mike's hands down to his sides. "Be good!"

"Always," he laughed.

As they approached the wedding party Mike took Jana's hand once again. She smiled at him and winked.

*****

The wedding, though only intended for close friends and family, appeared larger due to the venue. There were people milling around, watching the vows being exchanged. Sami's off-white, off-the-shoulder gown accentuated her long neck and spiked red hair. David's eyes never left his bride. They acted like they were the only couple ever to marry. The ceremony was brief, but it didn't take much to make it official. The hotel atmosphere that recreated Venice made it more elegant than could be imagined from such an open venue. Many people, tourists and hotel guests, joined in the festivity and wished the couple well.

As the wedding party got ready to leave Sami hugged her son. "Thanks for coming on such short notice, Charlie. I'm really happy you're here, and so is David." Sami gave Jana a big hug. "Thanks, Jana, I'm glad you're here too." Sami took Mike's hand, "I'm glad you're here as well young man. It makes you more part of the Brandon corporate family than you realize." Sami handed a check to Mike, here's your retainer. I hope the amount is correct. If not we can fix it next week when I return from my honeymoon." Mike took the check for $500K, glanced at it briefly, smiled, and placed it in his pocket. "I look forward to working with you."

"Thank you Sami-uh-ma'am. I look forward to meeting with your staff and working for your firm." Mike was in shock as he ran his hand over his breast pocket and felt the outline of the check. He could not contain his smile.

Charlie slapped him on the back. "Welcome to the family. You're going to find, I'm sorry to say, that working for my mom is much harder than working for Jana." His voice lowered to a conspiratorial whisper, "Besides, she's not as nice to look at."

Jana pinched Mike, "Are you in there?"

"I'm here; but I'm in shock. You knew this didn't you?"

"I won't lie to you. Sami told me this afternoon and asked if I wanted to tell you. As much as I did I thought it was better if she told you. I want you to know I had nothing to do with this, and Sami reminded me of that this afternoon as well. You did this on your own, and I'm very proud of you. This is what you were hoping for. It definitely starts your company in the right direction." She pulled him into a very suggestive and intimate kiss. "How about we go back to the room and start where we left off. If I remember correctly a very sensual young man started his evening with a cold shower. Maybe over the next few hours I can erase that terrible incident from your mind."

"I sort of thought we would enjoy the dancing, have a few drinks, party with the crowd," Mike joked.

"I'm game if you are," she tugged on his tie, "but don't ever say I didn't offer an—interesting—alternative."

"How about a compromise, I need to wind down a bit from the shock Ms Brandon just laid on me. As much as I hoped for the account I wasn't as confident as you were. I could use a couple of drinks. How about we slide into the bar at Delmonico's and you can have a couple of Pomegranate martinis and I'll have a couple of beers and we can see where the evening takes us from there. You game?"

"I'm game, let's tell Charlie good bye and get out of here."

"No, let's wave at Charlie from across the room and get out of here." As if Charlie heard he turned and saw them wave and leave the room.

Mike and Jana sat quietly in the bar and enjoyed their drinks. No glib conversation, in fact no conversation at all. Mike looked at Jana and smiled, "Want another drink?"

"Okay."

Mike raised his hand to signal the waitress to bring another round. Once received again, nothing.

Jana finished her second drink and stood up, "I'm going to the room, take a hot bath and go to bed. You stay and work this out in your mind. Three words to me in the last half hour tells me you don't need me to muddy the water here." She gave him a kiss and left the bar.

Mike watched her leave, and though he wanted her to stay he couldn't ask her to. *She's right, I need to work this out for myself.*

Jana pressed the elevator button, and as the door opened Charlie was standing there. She started to enter and he pushed her back, "No you don't. You look like you lost your best friend, what's up here? Where's Mike?"

"Nothing's up, I'm going up to take a hot bath."

"Alone, you're kidding right?"

"No, I'm not kidding. Look Charlie I'm tired and I want to relax. Mike is in the bar at Delmonico's trying to balance the world on his shoulder. I just spent the last half hour with him and he said exactly three words—'want another drink'—which were not very satisfying. I can't help him here, and though I might marry him if he asked me one more time, I don't think that's going to help either."

"Jana, you can't do that." Charlie pulled them to a corner, away from the crowds. "Neither one of you are ready to get married. You would grow to hate each other, you would hate him for making you give up your company, and he would hate you because you would no longer be the woman he fell in love with. Don't do anything crazy here. I'll talk to Mike. He just needs to sort it out. I hate to tell you this, but I'll be your escort home tomorrow. Mom wants Mike to stay here a couple more days and work out the logistics of moving his firm into her building. I know this isn't what you want to hear but you two being apart for a day or so won't be such a bad idea. It'll give you both some time. Okay, go up, take a hot bath and go to bed. I'm going to talk to Mike." Charlie kissed her on the forehead and pushed the button for the elevator. "It'll be okay, don't worry."

"Thanks, Charlie I really appreciate your help. Good night." The elevator door opened and she stepped in.

Ten

Charlie entered Delmonico's and saw Mike sitting alone, nursing a beer. *Jeez he looks worse than Jana did, here goes.* "Buy you another beer?"

"Charlie, good to see you, but no, I already had two, and if I intend to find our room I'd better not."

"Don't make me drink alone," Charlie raised his eyebrow, "I'm a good listener."

"Okay, one more but you have to at least agree to point me to the elevator. Without Jana I get really turned around in this hotel."

"I promise I'll get you to the right elevators." Charlie ordered two more beers. "What gives here Mike? I just saw Jana and she looked like she lost her best friend. What's going on with you two?"

"I asked her to marry me; I love her; your mom hired my firm to do her accounting work, Jana is the CEO of her own business and it isn't in Vegas. Guess that pretty much says it all." Mike shrugged his shoulders, holding up his palms questioning what to do.

"I can't make any choices for you, but maybe if you talk it through I can help line things up. First you're in love with Jana. That's really not surprising; I've been in love with her since I started to walk." Charlie sat back and paused, "I can't remember when she wasn't a part of my life. Even though Craig hired me, I stayed with the company when he left because of Jana. But loving her does not have to equate to marriage. Do you understand that? Love doesn't always result in marriage. If it did there would be a lot more divorces. What else?"

"I still love her, but okay. Your mom gave me the contract to do her accounting business. In fact, I have a fat ass check in my pocket to prove it. That's not bad; it just sucks as far as timing. You know when I began this affair with Jana three days ago I was pretty sure I could have an affair and walk away, but I don't want to. I have a huge opportunity on my door step and all I want to do is walk away. I mean, I could go home with her tomorrow and I know Mr. Nichols would give me a job without question. My only problem is that this offer, this opportunity is something I've been working for since I finished college. I don't want to give it up."

"Why would you even consider that as a viable option? Jana told you when this started that she wasn't looking for marriage, didn't you believe her?" Charlie raised his glass and drank down half his beer in one pass, he knew what was coming.

"Sure then, when she said it. But we hadn't spent the past couple days together. I didn't think it would be this good, and it's not just the sex, though that is fantastic. It's more, it's the way she makes me feel, and I know she feels the same. I would give anything if she'd be my wife."

"So you're willing to give up everything you worked for?"

"Yes," Mike said, "I am."

"That's crazy. She's no more ready to get married than you are. Though I want you to know, I think if you asked her again she'd say yes. But Mike, it would be one of the biggest mistakes you both made. Jana doesn't want to give up her company and move to Vegas, and you don't want to give up the opportunity you've been given, only to go back to working for someone else. Why should either of you? You're both consenting adults, you knew the plan going into this, and you both need to be honest about what you want. Jana was so proud of you this afternoon when mom told her she was going to hire you. She told her she wouldn't be sorry. She even staked her reputation on it. By giving up what you've been offered you not only hurt yourself, you'd hurt Jana. That's not any foundation for a healthy marriage."

Mike gazed around the bar, as if looking for the answer, "But I want Jana in my life. I know it's hard to believe, but I do love her."

"I know you think you do, but after three days I can't believe you have the type of lasting love needed to start a marriage. When you throw in the fact that one or both of you will walk away from something very near and dear to their hearts, it's almost like asking for the marriage to fail. You both need time on this marriage thing and you both need to take that time. Look at me," Charlie said. "If you truly love her, and she feels the same, it will be that way tomorrow and six months from now. Start up your business; get that going because if you intend to marry Jana you need to be able to support her in the style she's accustomed to. I doubt after a couple of days you even know what that means." Charlie smiled, "For example do you realize the dress she wore to my mom's wedding cost her $3,400? Are you really ready to take that on?"

The shock registered on Mike's face. "Shit! No, not really. I can't even imagine spending that much money on one item. You're right I had no idea. Jana and I definitely move in different worlds. I bet the shirt I have on cost more than everything else I'm wearing," he ran his hand over the luxurious fabric, "am I right?"

"Close, really close," Charlie laughed. "Mike, that's why you need to give this some time, time to get to really know the world she lives in, and what her expectations are. Having good sex doesn't give you an open window to her soul. Take the time to get to know each other. You'll still see each other. Your parents live in the same city as Jana, and Jana comes here three or four times a year. Take advantage of those meetings. Get to know each other as friends, and then decide your future. In the mean time you start your new company and let Jana run hers."

"Thanks, Charlie, for the counsel. Maybe I don't agree with everything you've said, but I know it's the right decision for now. I need to go up and talk to Jana, we need to work all this out and come to an understanding on the future."

"One more thing," Charlie said, "before my mom left, she told me that her foreman would be contacting you tomorrow and asking you to stay here a couple of days to work the logistics of your firm moving into their building. I told Jana I'd escort her home. She understands you need to do this, but I didn't want it to come as a surprise to you when you get the call in the morning."

"Appreciate it. Maybe staying on here for a couple of days would be good for both of us. I'll stay, I don't really want to because I really want to spend every minute I can with Jana before I leave, but I have to set my priorities, and getting my business situated is critical to my, to our, future." Mike stood, shook Charlie's hand, and left the bar.

That boy has a lot on his mind. I hope our talk helped give him some direction. The cougar is out, and I don't think it's a good idea for him to cage her so soon. Swallowing the last of his beer, Charlie rose and walked into the casino. *Time to lose some of my inheritance*, he smiled as he took a seat at a dollar slot machine.

*****

Mike unlocked the door of the room, it was completely dark.

"Mike, I hope that's you?" Jana whispered.

"It's me. Can I turn on a light? We really need to talk."

"Sure, turn it on."

Mike entered the room to find Jana setting on the sofa. He really expected her to be in bed. Actually he was glad she was up, it would have been harder to carry on this conversation in bed, it would've been a distraction. "I'm sorry about not talking to you earlier. I know you would've tried to help me sort through all this, but I needed to make these decisions on my own. I spent the last forty-five minutes in the bar with Charlie. He gave me some good counsel, but even with that I know the decisions I make now are mine alone."

Jana let him talk, "I'm listening."

"The last couple of days have been the best, and worst, of my life. I've fallen in love with the most beautiful woman, and I believe she cares for me as well. I've locked down a very lucrative future for a company I've been planning on since the day I entered college. I've had the greatest sex any one man could ask for." He smiled, "But even with all those things, to fully take advantage of them I've got to be willing to make some major sacrifices. I want to be with you Jana, forever." He saw her flinch, but he continued, "No, I know you would marry me if I kept pushing you, but I don't want to do that. If, and I say if, we ever marry I want it to be because you want to, not because you feel obligated to." Mike walked to the mini-bar and took out a bottle of water for Jana, and a beer for himself.

"Thanks," Jana said; she waited for Mike to get it all out before she responded.

"Leaving marriage out of the equation, it helps me concentrate on my business. I'm so happy, in fact ecstatic, about the possibilities I have with Brandon Inc. I couldn't have planned it any better. It gives me sufficient funds to stand up the business without having to borrow any money, it gives me great office space, and Sami—Ms Brandon—told me today in the meeting the firm she hired would be able to do work for other companies as long as they weren't major competitors. So I can pursue other business ventures as well and she'll still house my offices rent free as long as I work for her. I want to do this, I want to be my own boss and make a success of what I know best."

"Sounds like a great plan, but you seem reluctant to go forward."

Mike nodded, "I want you in my life Jana, I don't want the past few days to be a beginning and end to our relationship. That's the bottom line."

"It doesn't have to be an end to our relationship just because you're here and I'm not. I come here quite a bit, three or four times a year at a minimum. Your folks live where I do so I expect you'll travel to see them as well. This doesn't have to end, it just won't continue at the same pace." She laughed, "And mind you, I'm *not* complaining, but I'm not sure I could maintain this pace!"

Mike laughed as well. Jana's remark seemed to lighten the situation for him. "Charlie told me I was going to have to stay here a couple of days and work out the logistics for my company and that he would escort you home tomorrow."

"Yes, he told me. Mike, I understand. I'm a CEO as well. Sometimes, whether you like it or not, the company has to come first. If you don't understand that then you won't succeed. I guess that's the decision you have to make. If you want to follow your dream, you stay and get things set up."

"I want to stay. I want to get this company off the ground the right way."

"I'll fly home tomorrow, and when you get back in town next week, we can spend as much time together as we can before you have to return to Vegas. Did you give up your apartment?"

"Yes, I was planning on staying with my parents, but I haven't said anything to them yet."

"Tell you what, you come back and spend the last couple of days you're in town at my place. That way we can spend even more time together. You no longer work with my company, so it shouldn't create any more gossip than has already been started. Besides that your car is still in the shop. You can use my company car to take care of any last minutes things you need to do before you leave. How does that sound?"

"Almost too good to be true. You know when we began

this affair I thought it would be just great sex, slam bam thank you ma'am. It hasn't been. I'm in love with you Jana and I want you in my life. I want my company to be a success, and I know before I offer for your hand in marriage again I have to be able to support you in the style you're accustomed to."

"Well, not exactly. Mike, if, and it's a big if, we make the decision down the road to get married, I don't come to a marriage empty handed. I have a very large, very successful company as you know. If I decided to sell it outright I could live quite handsomely on the earnings of the reinvestments for the rest of my life, your life and then some. I've also considered moving my headquarters to Nevada for tax reasons. No I'm not making any hasty decisions right now. I need time to work all this out in my mind too. All that said, both of us need to concentrate on our individual CEO responsibilities." She yawned, "I'm tired can we sleep now?"

"Yes," he said reluctantly. He didn't want this to end without a commitment on Jana's part, but from her comments he knew she wasn't ready for that. She was probably right, and for now he would leave things as they were.

Jana climbed into bed and snuggled into Mike's arms. He held her tight and within minutes she felt his body totally relax in sleep. Smiling, she drifted off thinking how nice it was to have a man in her bed, *I've missed this intimacy, and if Mike leaves...*

*****

The normal, day-to-day office environment was exactly what she needed to put her life back on track. Las Vegas was exciting and her time with Mike had been wonderful. The reality now was work, and putting normalcy back into her daily routine, which always put a smile on Jana's face. Charlie was the perfect escort home and upon her arrival she had received a dozen red roses from Mike. The card simply stated, 'Miss you. Had a great time, wish you were still here, Mike', sweet but no love sonnet. She was a little disappointed, but she knew he was doing what he felt was best. She turned on her computer and glanced through her e-mails. Nothing that needed her attention right now, she could concentrate on the trip she was planning for next week to England and on to Egypt. It would've been nice to take Mike along, but that wasn't possible. She heard a knock on the door and looked up just as Charlie entered.

"How's it going this morning? You look good, the weekend must have been relaxing in spite of all the issues you and Mike encountered."

"It was a great weekend, and I truly enjoyed my time with Mike. I miss him, but I know he had things he needed to take care of." She saw Charlie's eyes narrow. "Don't look at me that way, I'm fine really. I know him staying there and me staying here is the best for right now. In the meantime you have a trip to plan for us. Also, Charlie thanks for escorting me home. I really appreciate you standing in for Mike."

"Wait a minute, back up. When you said we were taking a trip, you meant you're taking me with you?"

"That's my plan, unless you have some reason you can't go." She drummed her pen on her desk, "Do you?"

"Hell no, I can be packed in an hour."

"Excellent, but you're a few days too early, let's plan on leaving on Saturday morning and that gives us the weekend to get over the jet lag. Don't set up any meetings until Tuesday, and we can do some sightseeing if we have time on Sunday and Monday. I need to see Cheryl, if you'll ask her to stop by when she gets a chance this morning. I've got nothing on the calendar as far as meetings; in fact see if she wants to join me for lunch. If she does, go ahead and call and have it delivered for us, please."

"I'll take care of it. I noticed some traffic on that merger you were considering, you might want to read through the papers I left on your desk. There appears to be a couple of glitches that need to be worked before it can be finalized. You also might want to talk to Craig as his company is going to take on a small piece of the work as well."

"Okay I'll take a look." After Charlie left the office Jana sat back, turned her chair slightly and gazed out the window. The cityscape was beautiful. Big fluffy clouds hung from the sky like white sheets billowing on a clothes line. The mountains in the distance were hard granite she knew, but the sun casts shades of blue, lavender, pink and gold across the valleys. Yes, this is where she belonged. Turning slowly she picked up the folder Charlie left and began to read each and every word. Her phone buzzed and she picked it up.

"Mike's on line one," Charlie stated.

"Thanks," she pushed line one. "Hello handsome, how is your day going?"

"It'd be a lot better if you were here. I've met with Sami's folks and looks like I'll be on a plane day after tomorrow. My offices will be ready next week, but I'm not ready for any more people than my initial staff of five. I didn't call to talk about work. I miss you."

"I miss you too. I'm busy trying to arrange a trip to England and Egypt next week. I'm taking Charlie with me; he's excited. I'm leaving Cheryl in charge which will be a first for her too. I've got a merger I'm trying to finalize so I've got to make sure everything is as I want it to be. Other than that, I'm looking forward to spending a couple of evenings with you before you head back to Vegas. Oh, I wanted to tell you since you're coming in late I'll leave a key with the guard here and you can pick it up before you go to my condo. I've got a business meeting and I'm not sure I'll be back before you get there. I can't wait to see you, but I need to go now."

"I'll see you in a couple of days. Wish I was going with you to Europe."

"Honey, I wish you were too, in fact I was thinking the same thing not five minutes ago."

"Actually I find it hard already to concentrate on the business when I've got you so embedded in my mind."

"Snap out of it young man," Jana scolded. "You're a CEO, you have responsibilities. You have people counting on you. This is no longer about an accountant; this is about a company, a company depending on you to do the right thing all the time."

"Well that makes it easier," he laughed. "Don't help me anymore, okay?"

"I miss you, Mike, you do what you need to do, see you in a couple of days. Take care of yourself."

"Bye, Jana." *She's absolutely right, this isn't about me, it's about my company.*

Jana hung up the phone and stared at it; she hoped the days would pass quickly. She was looking forward to Mike coming back. She missed him.

*****

Lunch with Cheryl was always fun. She wasn't a picky eater, and though Jana knew she watched her weight, she would try anything. Jana and Cheryl had been close since Cheryl came to work for her over fifteen years ago. Now they were closer than ever with Cheryl being second in command. "I'm glad you could make lunch today, we've lot to talk about."

"Before we start with business," Cheryl smiled slyly, "tell me about this young man you've been courting around the square, so to speak.".

"Okay, he's started his own company in Vegas, which is where we went this weekend. He landed Brandon Inc. As his first client and he's there now trying to make all the arrangements and hire more staff."

"His first corporate client is Charlie's mom?"

"Exactly, I can't tell you what a convoluted mess that was." Jana explained the weekend's events, even telling Cheryl about Mike's marriage proposal.

"You're not going to get married—are you?" Cheryl's tone was more worry than questioning.

"Not any time soon. But it was nice he asked. I do care about him, but not quite in that way, which is what I told him. Hell, Cheryl, we both have companies to run and that's our immediate future. From there—who knows?" Jana sighed. "Okay, work issues. How are you coming with hiring the replacements behind Daryl and Mark?"

"I've done the interviews and we have a primary recommendation and an alternate for you to consider. I've brought the information with me so you could look it over. If you agree, we can make the offers and hopefully have both on board within the month. Both the primary and alternates are," Cheryl hesitated, "female. Do you think that will be a problem?"

"I don't think so, who was on your panel?"

"Julio from Inventory, Larry from Accounting, and me."

"Two males and a female on the panel, and all your primary selections are female." Jana bit her hip and nodded, "That does surprise me, but I guess it's really about time don't you think? Maybe that glass tower is beginning to shatter. I'll take a look at your recommendations and give you an answer before the day is out. Where are these folks working now?"

"The one I'm looking at for Daryl's position currently works for Craig." Cheryl watched Jana's face at the mention of Jana's ex. "He's not going to be happy, but she's good really good and she wants more independence, which I know we offer. The other is fresh out of school and has never worked anywhere. Yes, I see that look, but you need to meet her and talk to her. She's dynamic and will be great. She brings a young vitality to this firm. She's single, she's aggressive without being intimidating," Cheryl smiled, "hell, she reminds me of us when we first started."

"Tell you what, go ahead and make the offers. I'll look them over, but I'm comfortable you know what we need to make this company a success. I want them both on a year's probation just in case they don't fit. They don't cut it and we turn them loose, agreed?"

"I actually told them in the interview that was our policy, so it won't be a surprise. I'll hopefully know in the next couple of days when they'll start. I'll pass the info to Charlie."

"Good, I'll want to announce the selections to the firm before I leave next week. By the way, you're in charge while Charlie and I are in Europe. On a side note, get yourself an administrative assistant to help keep your schedule straight. I can't tell you how disorganized I'd be without Charlie. He's indispensable, and you'll find you won't know how you lived without one in the past. You can't cover all the administrative stuff and manage the company too," Jana made eye contact, "soon Cheryl, like by the end of the week. Charlie keeps a good contact list of these folks and can assist you in making a selection."

"OK," Cheryl agreed, "I'll take care of it." They finished their salads, enjoying each other's company talking about the trip to Europe and plans for the future.

*****

The next two days passed slowly. The dinner meeting was taking too long. She was distracted with Mike's arrival; she knew it, but she couldn't help herself. She caught Craig's eye and smiled.

"Jana," Craig asked, "do you have another engagement tonight?"

"Actually a friend is coming in and staying at my place, so I'd like to conclude this meeting and get home."

"I think we're done. You made the changes to the merger agreement and I've agreed, as has our attorney, so I guess we're done. I can stop by the office in the morning with the contracts for you to sign."

"Make it early afternoon," she smiled.

"I'll be there at one and we can put this one to bed." Craig patted the sheaf of papers, "This will make you a very rich woman."

"I'm already a very rich woman, but thanks for reminding me."

"How's that new boyfriend of yours?" Craig whispered.

"None of your business," she replied under her breath. She pushed back her chair, causing all the men at the table to stand. Jana smiled demurely, "Thank you gentlemen for your time. The food was great, the company even better. I look forward to working with all of you. Unfortunately, I've got another meeting," She turned and left the restaurant, immediately entering her waiting car for the ride home to Mike. Jana didn't hear the comments her dinner guests made to her ex-husband about Craig letting the best thing in his life walk away.

Entering her condo she called out, "Anybody here?"

"In here love," Mike answered. "How was your dinner meeting?"

"Long and tedious, and I was glad to put an end to it. We'd pretty much concluded the business part. The old men were sitting around enjoying their drink. I don't particularly care for that piece; it was something Craig always took care of. Since he was *there* I figured a good place for me was *here*." She walked to Mike and sat on his lap. She kissed him with a passion he felt was only for him. When she broke the kiss she smiled at him and brushed back his hair, "I've missed you."

"Lady, you don't know the half of it." He rose with her in his arms and carried her to the bedroom. He'd already turned the bed covers down and laid out a nightgown he knew she'd probably never get a chance to wear, at least not tonight. Running his hand along her thigh he felt the button of her garter belt. *God I missed this*. He assisted her in slowly removing her dress.

Jana leaned into him and felt his erection. *I can only be gracious and help him remove these cumbersome clothes. I know he's got to be uncomfortable.* She smiled to herself as she unfastened his belt and unzipped his pants. With little effort she had his pants down around his knees and his shorts followed next. She took his shirt in both hands and with a sexual hunger she'd never experienced she pulled hard and the buttons flew across the room. "If that's too aggressive," she purred, "let me know."

"Not a problem, gives me a reason to make you buy me a new shirt." Mike picked her up and placed her in the center of the bed. He needed to touch her everywhere. He kissed and caressed every crevice, wanting to make a memory of her body, something he knew he would fantasize about when they weren't together. "What time do you need to be in the office in the morning?" He nuzzled her neck.

"My first meeting is right after lunch. I'm all yours for the next twelve hours. Let's make the most of it." She pulled him down for the first kiss of many to come.

Mike teased her body, stroking her from her breasts to her stomach and lower, until he feared he could wait no longer. Easing his hand to the fork of her legs, he gently parted her nether lips and eased a finger inside. She was tight, but moist and ready for him. She rode his fingers, first one, and then two.

Jana marveled at the feelings his lightest touch stirred. Nerves she hadn't realized she possessed had been awakened, and the sensations fascinated and delighted her. Had anyone told her she could feel this way with any man, let alone one she had known for only a few days, she would never have believed it. She missed the intimacy shared with the opposite sex. They had come together only a short week ago, yet the bond they shared increased with each passionate coupling.

His hands felt as if they belonged on her body, stroking her, making her gasp again. As he slipped his erection inside, Mike began to move slowly, rhythmically. Jana savored each moment, focusing on each new sensation as he began to move faster and faster, plunging deeper with each stroke. Soon he was moving, quickly, powerfully. She blocked out even the slightest thoughts from her mind, wanting only to feel and be in the moment.

They collapsed and the room fell into silence. Mike murmured, "Are we dead?"

"No we're not dead," her hand brushed his penis and she felt him quiver at her touch, "can we do it again?"

"Are you trying to kill me?"

"No, death is the last thing on my mind. I just want to continue using and abusing you." She poked his arm, "You're young, where's your stamina?"

"I think you've been stealing it in pieces for the past couple of days. I'm going to need a month of R&R to regain my strength when I leave here this week."

"Does that mean this is it, no more sex before you leave? Do I need to bring in the substitutes?" she teased.

"Oh, there'll be more sex, as much as both of us can handle over the next couple of days. After I leave we can continue with phone sex, if you want."

"Phone sex doesn't sound all that satisfying, but I'm willing to trying anything—at least twice," she laughed.

"Woman, you are wearing me out." He laughed, the act shaking the bed, "But it's not something I would change for anything. Is there anything in particular *you* would like to do right now? Hmmm?"

"Like I said before, I'll try anything twice. Do you want me to direct the next skirmish, or do you want to throw the first blow?" She reached up and kissed him so hard his toes curled.

"Shit woman you're going to kill me, but what a way to die." He pulled her to him, hugging her tightly as he kissed her neck, nibbling on her ear lobe. They made love, quickly but passionately, talked of other things, made love again, talked again briefly and then a comfortable silence fell before Mike thought of something else he wanted to talk to her about. But, as he opened his mouth, he realized that the pattern of her breathing had changed to the shallow, even rhythm of sleep. *It can wait until tomorrow, I need sleep too.*

*****

At exactly 1229, Jana entered the office. She was dressed in her black Armani suit with a white lace camisole. She walked by Charlie's desk to pick up her messages. "Good afternoon, how are things going? Anything I need to be aware of?"

"Actually for a change things are quiet. Craig has called about twenty times this morning and he wouldn't leave a message. He needs to talk to you, but he said it wasn't pressing. To me his actions are counter to that position, but the only way to find out his problem is to give him a call. He wouldn't talk to me. He's on your calendar at one, so if you don't want to know sooner you can wait and talk to him then. Here are your messages, but like I said nothing pressing. I did give a couple to Cheryl and she took care of them."

"Okay, I'll wait for Craig to come to me. But…"

"What's up?"

"Nothing, just thinking. You're a man."

"Cute, what do you want to know?"

"This is Mike's last day, and I'd like to get him something, a going away gift."

"How about a Rolex?"

"Don't be obscene. I was trying to think of something that wasn't too personal, but would be something when he saw it or used it he would think fondly of me. Any ideas?"

"Well, since you don't like the idea of a Rolex, how about a nice pen and pencil set? You know, one of those Borsheim's Waterman Hemisphere Black Ball pen and pencil sets? I think the two would run a little over a hundred. I know a store in town that stocks them and they deliver. Would you want it engraved?"

"Actually that sounds nice, exactly what an upcoming entrepreneur could use. No, I don't want them engraved; I don't want them *that* personal. This way as he moves on in his life and his career he can use them without a guilt factor included. Call and have a set sent over. If they can't do it please go pick them up for me. I'm having dinner with him tonight and seeing him off tomorrow morning."

"I forgot to tell you that new accountant wants to see you." Charlie smiled a wicked smile, "I set up a meeting with him next week, but he wanted to see you today."

"Unless we are broke I don't want to see him until next week. If he still insists set him up a meeting with Cheryl. She can more than handle him."

"You are a wicked woman, but you're a picture in motion; I love watching the fish squirm when there's a shark in the water."

"Charlie, you've called me a cougar and now a shark. I think you're watching that Animal Planet channel too much."

"Well not sharks, no wait, yes a cougar with shark tendencies." He laughed as she walked away.

She turned, "Call the stationary store for the pens, and let me know when Craig gets here. Charlie, I'm not a shark, a cougar maybe, but not a shark." She laughed as she closed the door.

Jana waited for Craig to arrive. *I wonder what his problem is this time. His worrying gets old. Oh well, he'll be here in a couple of minutes and then I'll know.* There was a knock at the door and Charlie opened it to announce Craig.

Jana walked around her desk, gave Craig a kiss on the cheek and waved her hand to indicate he should take a seat. "So, Craig, Charlie said you've been calling all morning; what's up?"

"I don't know how to begin," he hesitantly replied.

"Craig, just tell me, you know I hate how you act coy and try to dodge the truth to keep from hurting me, or so you alluded over the course of our marriage. What's going on? Tell me quick or I'm going to have Charlie physically remove you from my office."

"I don't doubt he'd do as you asked, he always did," Craig whined.

"What's the matter with you?" Jana narrowed her eyes, carefully studying her ex-husband.

"Jana, over the next several months, and possibly for a year or so, I'm going to need your help with my company."

"*My* help? Help to do what for God's sake?"

"Help in the day-to-day operations."

"And I would do this...why?"

"Because you used to care about me, still do, at least I hope you do."

"Okay, enough of this crap. What the fuck is going on, Craig?"

"I just don't know how to begin, but here goes. I went to my doctor this morning and I've been diagnosed with prostate cancer." He watched her closely, waiting for a response.

She reached out and took his hand, "Craig, I'm so sorry. What is the doctor's prognosis?"

"Actually he feels good that he caught it in the early stages. They're going to do some more tests and a couple of biopsies of the lymph nodes, and they'll decide a course of action to fight the progress of the disease. He's even looking at removing the prostrate as he says I don't really need it, but that will be a last resort. The doctor believes with chemotherapy, some radiation treatments and monitoring they can stay ahead of it. Unfortunately the treatments are going to take me out of operation for a couple of months. Based on what I was told I shouldn't have a problem working during the radiation treatments though. If we go to surgery, then we'll have to take it a day at a time. That's why I'm here." He stood and handed Jana some legal looking documents.

"What are these for?"

"They give you full power of attorney to do anything you need to do to keep my company operational if I become ill. There's also a medical power of attorney to get care for me as needed if I'm incapacitated, and a living will so the hospital doesn't keep me alive by plugging me into a lot of useless machines. If anything, and I know you know this, if it's my time to go I want to do it with dignity. Lastly is a copy of my will which leaves everything to you and Liza, with you making the decision on who gets what."

"Craig I appreciate your trust in me, but as always you failed to consider whether I'd even be willing to do this or not. Don't you think Liza would do this for you better? She's your daughter and she loves you."

"I know, but I don't think she could run the business, and that's one of my biggest concerns. If you have oversight I know you'll do what's best since a lot of what I do, we do together in joint efforts."

Jana cast a glance at the picture of their daughter on her desk, "Have you told Liza?"

"Not yet, I wanted to talk to you first."

"Do you want to call her now, so we can all three discuss this?"

"I'd like to wait until the rest of the tests are back. That way we'll know a plan of attack and exactly what we're up against. Jana, if you don't want to do this I'll understand, really I will."

"You know I'll do this for you, and I'll stand by you, but we need to get help. I've got some European commitments to personally attend to. Hopefully I'll get most of the standup of those efforts accomplished while you're waiting for the test results, but if not we need a plan."

"I really appreciate your help with this, I really didn't know who else to ask."

"What about your girlfriend, what's her name—Candice?"

"Unfortunately the minute she found out about this and the potential that I'd need my prostrate removed, meaning no further sex, she walked. To tell you the truth I wasn't surprised, I knew how shallow she was, even though you didn't think so." He smiled shyly.

"Craig, let's agree that our respective love lives are off limits for discussion. Listen, I've got another meeting, but we'll talk more about this tomorrow. Why don't we have dinner tomorrow night?"

"Sure, I guess, what about Mike?"

"Even though I told you just a minute ago we weren't going to discuss our respective love lives, I'll answer your question. Mike leaves in the morning for his new job in Vegas. No more questions, as I don't want to lie to you." She kissed him softly and gave him a hug as she escorted him to the door. "I'll call you later tomorrow to set up dinner plans." Closing the door, she leaned back against it and began to cry. *Damn I feel like the Godfather, 'every time I think I'm out they pull me back in'.* She walked to her desk and took a tissue from the drawer to blow her nose. *Shit.*

Jana looked up as Charlie knocked and entered her office. "What was Craig's problem this time?" He saw her tear stained face.

"It's not good. He was diagnosed with prostate cancer."

"Oh my God, what's he going to do?"

"His doctor is doing more tests, and then they'll develop a plan." She handed Charlie the legal documents Craig had given her and waited for him to finish reading them. "I know he's left me in control of his life once again, but I couldn't say no and he knew I wouldn't. Damn, Charlie I thought I was out of this."

"Jana, you are out of it. You care for him as a friend, and that's not going to change; hell, he's the father of your only child. But this is a business arrangement, nothing else. Don't let him do this to you. His *poor Craig, nobody loves me* routine has lost its appeal. What happened to his little honey, what's her name Calamity?"

"No," Jana chuckled, "it's Candice and she's split. This

entire sickness thing was too much for her to handle. In some ways I can't blame her, as I'd like to do the same thing."

"You won't, you'll stick. Does Liza know?"

"Not yet, Craig wants to wait until he has more of the medical results and a plan forward. I'm thinking of calling her anyway so she can start figuring out how much she wants to get involved. You know her husband is in Iraq right now, so she could actually come here and live with her father while all this is going on. In fact, I bet her husband would like it if she was here versus staying at the base. She hasn't been working lately, so she's free if we need her. I think it's a good idea, and I'll talk to Craig about it tomorrow night at dinner."

Charlie grimaced, "Jana don't get tied to that man again, it isn't healthy for you."

"Don't worry, I won't, but with Mike leaving tomorrow I think I'll need someone to talk to and Craig is as good as anyone."

"To hell with Craig, let me get you a dog, or something that won't borrow your car or your money."

"Thanks, I think. Get out of my office, I've got some planning to do for our trip next week. Yes we're still going. If push comes to shove with Craig, I'll pay for Liza to come and stay to help her dad while we're in Europe. Is that better?"

"Yes, at least you're thinking about your needs first versus his. I think he's using you, as is his normal way of doing things. Just be careful, okay."

"I know he's using me Charlie, but what can I do? I'll be careful-and Charlie," she hesitated.

"Yes..."

"Thanks for watching out for me." She smiled and watched him leave her office. She dialed Mike's cell. It rang and rang but there was no answer. She left a voicemail, "This is Jana, call me at the office if you get a chance, otherwise I'll see you tonight, nothing urgent." *I just need to talk to someone who actually puts me first, damn it I didn't need this to complicate my life right now.* She dialed another number and Jana waited for Liza to answer.

"Hello," came the lazy response with a radio playing loudly in the background.

"Hi sweetheart, how're you doing?"

"I'm fine. Aren't you at work? Is something up?"

"Yes and yes. Are you sitting down?"

"Mom, what's the matter. Has something happened, is dad okay?" Liza questioned, desperate to hear her mother's response.

"Liza, your dad got some bad news this morning from his doctor."

"Wait mom, let me turn the stereo down; I can barely hear what you said." All Jana could hear was the music and then nothing, the line went dead. "Mom are you there? What did you say?"

"Liza, now don't panic, listen to all I tell you. Okay?"

"Yes mom, just tell."

"Your dad went to his doctor today and he was diagnosed with prostate cancer. As of right now they are still running tests, but the doctor feels they caught it early and he thinks with radiation treatment and possibly some chemo, your dad will be fine. We won't have a good plan until probably next week when he gets the tests all back. Okay, asks your questions and I'll try to answer them."

"Mom why didn't dad call me?" she was hurt her father hadn't made that single effort.

"Honey, he didn't want to worry you and he felt if we waited until next week when we had a more definite plan that it would be best for you. I knew you would be mad if you knew we'd known for a week and hadn't said anything to you, so that's why I called. If your dad gets mad at me, so be it."

"What do you need me to do?"

"Nothing right now and that's partly why I called. Last week when we talked, I told you Charlie and I were making a trip to Europe. I can't put that off any longer, and even though your dad says he needs me here I have to go to Europe to take care of business. It can't wait. If you don't mind, I'd like you to come and stay here until I get back. I know your dad is too proud to ask, but I know he'd feel better if you were here, and I definitely would feel better since I can't be here. Do you mind?"

"No, I don't mind I'm not doing anything anyway with Jake in Iraq. In fact if dad wants, I can work for him and stay close if he needs me. Do you think that's doable? I'd love to earn a little money while I'm there."

"I'm sure he'd like that, and if not then you can come and work for Cheryl. In fact she's looking for an administrative assistant right now and you'd be great as temporary fill until she finds exactly who she wants. You can even stay with me or your dad whatever works best for you."

"Mom that's great. Should I call dad?"

"You can, I know he'd love to hear from you. He might actually be happy all this is out in the open and he isn't the one that had to tell you. You know how much he hates being the bearer of bad news. Tell him your plans, and we can work the details out over the weekend. I love you. Talk to you soon."

"Bye mom; love you too. I'm calling dad and giving him a ration of shit. Silly old man," she laughed. "Bye mom, talk to you soon."

Jana laid down the phone just as her cell rang. "Jana, here, may I help you?"

"In more ways than one sweet lady," Mike drawled. "Got your message and wanted to see if you were going to be late, or we needed to meet somewhere versus the condo."

"No, I'll meet you there at seven. Did you get a chance to stop by your parents?"

"Yes, I took mom to lunch and spent the afternoon with dad in his shop. I told them a little white lie. I said I was leaving tonight and would call them tomorrow evening."

"I understand. I've got a few things to finish so I'll see you tonight. I miss you."

"I miss you too. Love you."

Jana smiled as she put her cell back in her purse. *I'm going to really miss that young man, he makes me feel so special. Could there ever be anyone else that will make me feel that way?*

*****

As they left for the airport the stillness was deafening. Talk to me, just talk to me. "Do you need anything for the trip, magazine, gum?" she questioned softly.

"No, I'm fine." He turned and took her in his arms. "Come with me Jana, we can make this work. I know we can."

"Honey, we've talked this to death. You know I can't do that. I've got a business to run, I've got a trip to Europe to complete and there's the problem with Craig. I promised I'd help him." She saw the stricken look on his face, "Mike please don't make this harder than it already is." She lifted his chin to look in his eyes. "Tell you what, let's plan to get together a month from today, whatever Friday that is. I'll come to Vegas and get a room at the Venetian. You can come and stay with me and we'll pretend no one else exists. What do you say?"

"Actually doesn't sound all that bad, but I don't think I can wait that long. I'm really going to miss you. This week has been fabulous and to tell you the truth I'm afraid."

"Afraid of what?"

"I guess that you won't come. You really mean it right, in a month, it's a date? I'm going to mark the days on my calendar. You'll really come?"

"In more ways than one I hope," she laughed. As they pulled up to the departure gates Mike prepared to leave the limo. "Wait I have something for you." She reached into her purse and pulled out a wrapped package.

"I've got something for you too." He withdrew a beautifully wrapped box from his briefcase.

"Okay, on three, we'll open them together. One, two, three." Jana began to open her present while Mike opened the one she'd given him.

Mike said, "Oh Jana, these are so elegant. I've looked at different sets for a while now but these are exquisite. Whenever I use them I'll think of you."

"Thanks, sweetheart that was exactly my plan." She finished opening her package. Enclosed was a very beautiful, small porcelain box with blooming Iris on top and Petunias at their base. Jana knew it was a Limoges box as she had many in her collection. The mere fact that this young man, in just a short week, knew her love of Iris and small boxes amazed her. Tears filled her eyes as she opened the box and found her favorite Licorice Jelly Bellies inside. There was no holding back the tears, "Oh, Mike, you are the most precious individual I've ever met. I can't tell you what this means to me. You make me feel so special. God, I'm going to miss you." She threw her arms around his neck meeting him in a very passionate, wet kiss.

Steven, the driver, waited the appropriate moments and then opened the door to help Mike out. Jana joined him, still crying. "Stay in touch, remember I'm only a phone call away. Good luck with your new business."

"I love you Jana, don't ever forget that." Mike gave her one more crushing hug, kissed her deeply and then walked into the terminal.

As much as Jana wanted to go with him she knew she couldn't. Steven helped her back into the car, and as they proceeded to drive away Jana turned in the seat and saw Mike looking at her through the window. She waved frantically and he waved back. *I miss him so much already.* Steven started to open the window between the seats, but heard her crying and closed it as he merged into traffic. *I'll give her a few minutes to compose herself, then see where she wants me to take her.*

About fifteen minutes later the window came down and Jana spoke, “Steven, take me to the office please.”

“Yes, Ma’am.”

She had a trip to plan, a merger to complete, she was having dinner with Craig, and Liza would arrive tomorrow. She wiped her eyes, blew her nose and whispered out loud, “I need this trip…Europe here I come.”

End

The Story Continues

In

Cougar Bounty

Cougar Bounty

I only like two kinds of men, domestic and imported.
Mae West

Cougar: "A new breed of single, older women. A cougar is a beautiful animal: sleek, powerful and in control. Being a cougar is an attitude, not a number." (Valerie Gibson, author of *Cougar: A Guide for Older Women Dating Younger Men*)

One

Jana moaned and arched her back. The flickering candles cast her surreal silhouette on the cave walls, her flowing hair, her proud breasts. She grabbed his long black hair in her hands, twisting it, pulling herself to him. She rose—and descended—again, riding a wave of passion. He was not the first and would not be the last. She looked down on him, and watched in horror as her hands changed, from the creamy skin, to something brown, tawny, her fingers contracting, the nails becoming claws. Her golden eyes blazed and she snarled...

SHIT! Jana threw off the covers and sat straight up in bed. The room was black, save for the soft green glow from the clock, 3:30 a.m. She shook her head, *a dream, I was...*when she rubbed her eyes her hand came back wet. She looked at her night gown; it clung to her damp body. *Damn, that was weird.*

*****

It was noon and in spite of the time of day, the airport was quiet, very few people meandering around the entrance. Jana approached the waiting area watching passengers funnel through the access gate with no sense of hurry in their step. She scanned the faces, looking for Liza. As she waited the week's events played over and over in her mind. Craig had cancer and Liza was coming to help with her dad's care. *There she is, as beautiful as ever.*

Jana approached, hugging her tightly. "It's great to see you honey; how was your flight?"

"Crowded, seems like every red-neck in the country was on that flight." That slanted grin her daughter was famous for eased the corners of her mouth into a welcome. "How's dad?"

"He's good; we can only assume no news is good news. He's going to be surprised to see you."

"No he won't; I told him I was coming, even though he said it wasn't necessary."

"Really! Obviously he didn't know what he was talking about, as usual."

"Mom, you need to behave. We need to give him the benefit of the doubt for now."

"Oh no you don't; he's not getting off that easy." Jana proceeded to baggage claim, "Let's get your luggage."

Liza stopped short, "Mom, this is all I have."

"It can't be; I thought you were going to stay for a while." Jana placed her hands on her hips, turning to Liza in her 'I'm your mother' stance, demanding answers.

Liza rolled her eyes, "Don't worry Mom; the rest of my stuff will arrive by UPS the first of next week. I saw no reason to drag all that through the airport." Liza caught their reflection in the mirror above the rental car company. They were very similar and could pass for sisters versus mother and daughter. Though Liza's hair was longer, reaching her waist, the dishwater blonde color was the same. They were the same height, five seven, with voluptuous yet curvy female figures. The most noteworthy trait they shared was their dazzling green eyes.

"You had me worried; I thought you'd changed your mind about helping out. What are you looking at?"

"Us," Liza shook her head, "never mind, let's go." Back in sync with her mother, Liza grumbled as she approached the exit. "I would've preferred bringing everything with me, but this was easier. By the way, thanks for the ticket, though it would have been nicer if it'd been first class."

"Stop, with the last minute purchase that wasn't possible."

"Do you think I'm getting snobbish, mom?"

Jana hooked her arm in Liza's and walked to the limo. "Not snobbish, maybe spoiled."

"Look who's talking," Liza wagged a finger at the long black car, "a limo mom, really."

"I could've brought Charlie's Mini."

"Yea right, like that was a possibility. Charlie would never let you drive his baby."

"That's true."

As she slid into the limo, Liza turned, "Mom, I'm glad you came to pick me up. Are you off the rest of the day or do you need to go back to the office?"

"I'm the boss; I gave myself the rest of the day off. If you want, we can drive over and see your dad, or we can go over tomorrow."

"Let's wait until tomorrow." Liza placed her duffle bag at her feet. "Nothing's going to change that fast, besides I wanted to get your opinion on a couple things first."

"Like what exactly?"

Liza took a deep breath, "I want to run dad's company."

"You know your dad's not going to understand you wanting to be boss."

"I know, but if I have a solid plan, one he'll agree to, then I know I can convince him this is the right answer." Liza ran her hand across her stomach as it grumbled, "I'm starving; can we stop and get something to eat?"

"Sure what are you hungry for?"

"I'd really like a nice green salad with fried chicken on

top. I know, not too healthy but it sounds good. Dad was telling me that there were a lot of new restaurants around the Mall. Are any of them good?"

"Yes there's one called Brava and they make an excellent Romano-Crusted Chicken salad." Jana lowered the window to her driver, "Please take us to Brava."

Liza relaxed into the leather seats, "Charlie said you were getting out, seeing younger men."

"I did go out a few times with a young man." Jana removed her glasses and repeatedly cleaned the lenses. "And *what* is Charlie doing discussing my personal life with you? I'm going to have a talk with that young man."

"Leave Charlie alone, he did nothing wrong."

At their destination the driver opened her door. "We're here, Ms Gates. Do you want me to wait, or do you want to call me when you're ready?"

"How about you come back and get us in an hour?" Jana said. "That should give us plenty of time to relax, have a couple of drinks and a nice lunch."

The waiter guided them to a secluded booth. Once seated Jana saw the worry in her daughter's eyes, "I guess I'm just worried. Come on, Liza; I'm not that bad." Jana looked at the menu, "What looks good to you?"

Liza grinned at her mother's antics. She was avoiding discussing whatever was bothering her. *Okay I can wait.* "I'll have a salad, then I won't feel guilty when I have desert; how about you?"

"I think I'll do the same." When the waiter returned with their drinks, a martini for Jana and soda for Liza, Jana ordered two salads.

"Okay mom; start talking, what's going on with you?"

Jana glanced around the room, avoiding her daughter's gaze, "I know this is selfish, and I'm only thinking about myself, but I hate this thing with your dad."

"You mean the cancer? That's not dad's fault."

"No, I don't mean the cancer; I realize he has no control of that. What I hate is all the legal documents he had drawn up without talking to me-or you. And then me, dumb me, I agreed to everything, which he knew damn well I would. He played on my sympathy just like he always has." She slammed her hand on the table. "The fact that I let him manipulate me yet again infuriates me."

"I know mom," Liza reached over and laid her hand on Jana's, "I wasn't happy about it either. I have a solution. Let's have all the papers redone-with me in control. What do you say?"

"I say yes. That's exactly what needs to be done. It would leave you in full control and if, and only if, you need help, you can call me; how does that work for you?"

"Actually, I like that arrangement. Now all we have to do is convince dad." Liza sighed; she knew it would take a major offensive to convince her father. "But mom, I'd get really pissed if every time we talked you billed me for the conversation."

Jana laughed, "As lucrative as that might be, I wouldn't do that." She sipped her pomegranate martini, "When do you intend to start working?"

"As soon as dad gets all the papers changed. Until then I'm just visiting. You know as well as I do if I start work under the current arrangement, he'd never change a thing; there'd be no reason to."

"Boy, do you have him pegged," Jana teased. "I can't wait; can I be there when you tell him?"

Liza took a deep breath, "This isn't going to be easy for him." She paused and a silence fell over the table as she ran her finger around the rim of her glass. Looking her mother in the eye, she softly voiced her father's wish. "Dad told me the other night that he'd made a mistake in divorcing you. He wants you to come back to him and I'm thinking he feels because he needs you now that you will." Liza watched the turbulent emotions cross her mother's face.

Jana took Liza's hand. "Honey, you know that's *not* going to happen don't you? I don't want to be married, and I definitely don't want to be married to your father." She watched Liza take a deep breath. "Stop that, it's not that I don't care about his health, I do, but I'm not sacrificing *my* health for his."

Liza squeezed her hand, "I'm fine mom; we have a solid plan. Do you want to drive over to dads after lunch and discuss it with him, or wait until tomorrow?"

"I think tomorrow's soon enough, in fact I'll call your dad's attorney when we get home and have him meet us at dad's with all the paperwork. You'll have to convince him this is the right thing to do; think you can do that?"

"Me?" Liza's eyes widened, "You're going to help me aren't you?"

"Yes, I'll help you, but you need to let him know that you won't stay and help him unless he makes these changes. If you don't hold firm he won't change the documents, or he'll keep putting it off thinking you'll change your mind."

"I can do this mom, I can run dad's firm."

"I've no doubt; otherwise I wouldn't have called you. Let's talk about something else. What do you hear from Jake?"

"He's doing fine, counting the months until he comes home. He was glad to hear I was going to move back here. He wanted to come and work for dad when he got out of the service and me moving here begins that process."

"I need another drink, how about you?"

"Sure, fine I'll take another soda."

"I need something stronger." Jana raised her hand to get the waiter's attention. "He's cute, don't you think?"

"Who? The waiter? Yea, I guess he's okay."

"He's more than okay, take a closer look. Wouldn't you like to just eat him up?"

Liza took Jana's drink, "That's enough alcohol mom; you're acting crazy. You remind me of one of those cougars I used to work with."

"Cougar," Jana paused and leaned back in the booth, "interesting word; that's what Charlie calls me."

"Mom, I thought Charlie was pulling my leg, but you *really are* dating younger men, aren't you?"

Jana's eyes twinkled, "Define *younger*."

"I'll take that as a definite yes. I guess conceptually I don't have a problem with it. Hell dad's been living with Bambi, right? I don't see why you can't do the same thing."

"Her name is *not* Bambi. It's Candice, you sound like Charlie. I think he called her Calamity the other day. And Candice split with the arrival of your dad's medical problem."

"Whatever mom, it doesn't really matter what her name was, right? She's split so it's not something I have to remember."

"Liza, I did date a very nice young man, he was about your age. He left for a job in Vegas. So I'm not exactly like your dad, I haven't moved anyone in with me. But I'll be honest; I didn't realize how much I truly missed not having a man in my life." Jana laughed when she saw Liza's pained face, "Okay, I won't talk about my sex life anymore; I know that makes you crazy. But I do have a question. You don't think less of me, do you?"

"No mom, let's pay the bill and go home. I'm sure the driver's waiting for us."

As they entered the condo Jana walked to the phone. "I'll call the attorney and then I need a nap." She dialed the number from memory. Liza listened to the one sided conversation.

"James, this is Jana—Yes, it's been a long time—No, there's nothing wrong—James, you know all the papers you drew up this week for Craig? Well I need you to redo them with my daughter Liza as the primary on all the documents—Yes, Craig agrees—Can you meet us tomorrow at Craig's at 1100 so we can resign everything?—Yes Liza is here—See you then, thanks, James.

"He'll meet us there. He tried to convince Craig to do this originally and was really happy he'd come to his senses." Jana shrugged, "OK, so your dad hasn't come to his senses, *yet*. All you have to do is make that happen before he arrives tomorrow." Jana hugged Liza and walked to her bedroom. "If I'm not up in a couple of hours wake me, otherwise I won't sleep tonight." Closing the door, she lay down and covered herself, falling into a deep sleep.

Two

Her feet hit the floor as Jana grabbed her pounding head. *Damn, I feel like hell. I only had two drinks.* "Liza, are you here?" she called as she walked into the living room.

"I'm in the den."

As Jana entered Liza surveyed her mother's disheveled appearance. "You look like you got hit by a truck."

"Actually, other than a headache I feel okay." Jana watched the disapproval in her daughter's look. "I'm sorry if I embarrassed you."

"You didn't mom, I'm fine with you being you." She handed Jana a scrap of paper with a name and a phone number.

"What's this?"

"That's the name and number of our waiter. He said you should give him a call."

"Oh God, I don't even remember him."

"I recommend you not go back to that restaurant for a while. I'm sure their help turns over rather quickly." Laughing, Liza stood and hugged her mom. "You're a trip. So what do you want to do for dinner? Do you want to stay home, order something to be delivered, or do you want to cook."

Jana narrowed her eyes at her daughter, "Why, don't you cook?"

"That means we're having macaroni and cheese, or did you forget my cooking skills are very limited."

"You're right; I forgot. Let's order in; how about Chinese?"

"I'll take care of it. Do you want what you usually order, or do you want to try something different."

"Same as usual will be great."

Jana waited impatiently for Liza to finish dressing. "I know we aren't on a time schedule, but if you don't put it in high, Craig's attorney is going to get there before we do and that won't be good for any of us."

"Okay, I'm ready, let's go." They grabbed their purses and walked to Jana's limo.

"Good morning Steven," Jana said, "we need to go to Craig's and we're late, so anything you can do to make up some time would be appreciated."

"Yes, Ma'am, we should be there in about ten minutes if traffic cooperates."

"That's great." Jana turned to face Liza, "Are you ready for this?"

"Yes, mom, I've got a plan. I want to talk to him alone if you don't mind."

"I think I need to be there with you. I promise I won't say a word. Trust me, I know your dad and if he doesn't think I'm backing you from every direction he'll keep giving you reasons why everything should stay the way it is." Jana noted Liza's doubting expression, "I promise not to say a word."

"Okay mom, but I want to do the talking. If I can't convince him, then it won't happen," she looked out the window, "and we'll have to go to option two."

Jana raised her eyebrows, "What's option two?"

"Actually I don't have an option two, so option one has to work." They both laughed.

As the car approached Craig's condo Jana closed her eyes, saying a silent prayer. *God, please help Liza, she's going to need your intervention here to convince her dad. I know if Craig will just listen, he'll agree.* The car door opened and she looked up, *Show time.*

Craig rushed out, hugging Liza to his chest. "Oh honey, it's good to have you here. I've missed you so much. Jana it's good to see you too." He leaned over and kissed Jana's cheek. "Come in ladies, I've got refreshments on the terrace."

"Dad, the gardens are spectacular," Liza exclaimed as she took a seat at the table.

"Thanks honey, I take care of the ones by the house, but I have a gardener who handles the beds around the back and along the fence line. Since I own the condo complex, I got to play a role in the garden designs. I've really enjoyed working with the landscapers. Do you garden at all, Liza?"

"No, dad, not my thing, I'm not an outdoors type. Jake does some when he's home, but I can't keep plants alive." She took a deep breath, "Dad, I bet you're wondering why mom and I came over this morning."

"Well, I never gave it much thought. I figure you were here to see me, since your *mom*," he glared at Jana, "couldn't keep her mouth shut about my cancer. I knew you'd come."

"Let's not go there dad. I'm really angry with you for not calling me. I'm not a little girl any more who needs protection. I can handle the bad stuff just like any other grown up."

"I know honey, but it's hard for me to think of you as other than my little girl." He took her hand in his.

"Dad, we need to be serious here. I have something to say and I want you to listen and, if possible, I'd like you not to say anything until I'm done."

"I can't talk? That doesn't seem fair," he teased.

"Dad, I need your word you won't interrupt."

"Okay, I agree. I'll listen and when you're done hopefully you'll let me talk."

Liza took a deep breath, "When mom called me the other day and told me you had been diagnosed with prostate cancer, I was angry. Why angry you ask; because you didn't call me." Pausing to see his reaction and finding none, she continued, "You have always avoided telling me anything unpleasant. You tended to leave it to mom while you were married, but since you aren't married any more, you should have called me." Reclining in her chair, she took a drink of her ice tea. "That's off my chest, let's get down to business."

"That wasn't it?"

"No, I'm not done. No!" She held up her hand to keep him from continuing. "You promised you wouldn't talk," she scolded him and laughed. "Okay back to the business at hand; I want you to change the legal documents you had drawn up that left mom in charge of your company. I want you to put me in charge. I've worked for you both since I was sixteen and I know you've been pleased with my performance. I know how the business is run and I can handle it dad, I know I can. To help, I've asked mom to be an on-call consultant, but the oversight of your company would fall to me." She waited for him to respond.

Craig looked at Jana, "Do you agree with her?"

"Absolutely, Liza is more than capable of handling this, and I won't be that far away if she has any problems. You have a strong senior staff and they will help her when needed. If she has questions, I'm but a phone call away." Her eyes met Craig's, "And it does still keep the business in the family."

"But, Jana, you agreed to do this. I see no reason to make this type of change," Craig crossed his arms and stubbornly raised his chest in defiance.

'Dad, don't talk to mom like I'm not here," Liza snapped. "I want you to do this for me. It's what you've been promising me for years. By giving this to mom, you're telling me I'm not ready."

"Liza, that's not what I'm saying. You're ready, but you don't live here. Your mom is here all the time."

"You're wrong dad, I do live here. I moved into mom's condo yesterday and I intend to stay here to help you-if you let me. Of course if you don't want me to work for you then I'll go to work for mom until Jake gets back from Iraq."

"You've moved here, but why?"

"Because mom asked me to dad, is that so hard to understand? She feels she needs my help to run your business. Why don't *you* think so?"

"I just didn't think you'd come."

"You didn't ask me, so how would you know?" Liza gritted her teeth and continued. "Look, dad, you need to decide, do you want my help or not. If not, that's fine I can deal with that. If you do, you need to put it in writing."

"I'm sorry honey." He sighed; his shoulders fell, "I know I didn't handle this well. I'll do whatever I need to set this right, I promise."

The doorbell rang and Liza looked at Jana and smiled. "Actually, dad, you don't have to do that. James is at the door with the documents you need to sign."

"How do you know that?"

"Dad, get real. Mom called him last night; told him what we wanted done and invited him here today. She had him make the changes needed to the documents you had drawn up."

"You were pretty sure of yourself young lady," her dad squeezed her fingers.

"Dad, just so you know. If you'd have said no, I'd have never spoken to you again," forcing a smile, she squeezed his fingers in return.

"Liza, you know I love you and I'd never hurt you. I wanted to settle this quickly and because you weren't here I opted for your mom."

"Thanks a lot," Jana replied snidely.

"Jana, you know I didn't mean it that way."

"Yea, right; you, as usual, took advantage of me and the sympathy I'd have for your problem. But, we don't have to go there any longer since you're going to make the changes we know you *should* have made to begin with. Even James said he tried to tell you, but you wouldn't listen."

"Let's welcome James and get this over with." Craig's housekeeper led James onto the terrace.

"Good morning everyone, I hope I'm not late."

"No James, you're right on time, can I get you something to drink?"Craig was the ever ready host.

"No, thanks; I have an engagement with my family. I need to get this completed as quickly as possible."

As James laid out the papers, Craig signed them.

"Craig, I'll have these notarized and back to you in the morning with copies for Jana and Liza as well."

"That's fine James," Craig stood and shook his hand, escorting him to the door.

"What do you think mom, do you think he's mad at us?"

"Us no, me yes; your father doesn't like it when I get him to do things he doesn't want to do. He's feeling like we ganged up on him."

"Don't you think he knew this is exactly what we'd do?"

"Sure he knew, and I think he's been waiting for us to come here. I believe the old fool did this to bring us all back together. Like a family, if you know what I mean."

"Why would he do that mom?"

"When he came to my office I got the feeling from his comments that he wanted to get back together, that he was sorry we'd separated. Hell, you confirmed that yesterday, but it's too late."

"Is it too late Jana?" Craig asked as he walked back onto the terrace and took his seat.

"Yes, it's too late. I love you Craig, but not the way you

need to love a person you want to be married to. We're nothing but good friends now, and that's all there can be. Since this is settled I've got bags to pack for my trip." Jana stood, "Liza do you want to stay with your dad, or go home with me?"

"I'll stay for a while if you don't mind. I'll take one of dad's cars or maybe I can sweet talk him into giving me a ride."

"Okay, I'm out of here. Craig thanks for everything, I think you made the right decision. Liza, see you later." Turning, she walked into the house. *It's good when a plan comes together.* Jana relaxed and thanked her lucky stars she had the daughter she did. *Packing, all I need to do is pack. I'll spend a quiet evening with Liza, board my plane tomorrow with Charlie and have a great trip. That's exactly what I need, concentrating on my job and my company, that's what's important right now.*

Three

Jana boarded the plane, taking her seat. She didn't know where Charlie had gotten off to, but she knew he'd arrive soon. Sure enough, she looked up and saw him board. He took his time, flirting with each of the flight attendants as he moved toward her. Laughing and smiling, he sat down.

"So many women, so little time," he muttered under his breath.

"You're such a sleaze Charlie, grow up will you," she laughed, enjoying the respite from all her personal problems. "Where'd you go?"

"I wanted to pick up a few essentials for the trip. He took several small bottles of alcohol from his bag and put them in the seat pocket in front of him. "These are for later, they'll help us sleep. I also picked up a few snacks and a great sandwich we can share."

Jana rolled her eyes, "Charlie, we're in first class; they feed us more often than they do in a hospital. Alcohol is free and you can get as blitzed as you want."

"I know," he whispered, "but this is better because we aren't supposed to bring it on board; it's contraband."

"If they *see* it they'll confiscate it."

"Then we need to start drinking it immediately." When the flight attendant brought them both coffee and a glass of tomato juice Charlie filled both the coffees to the brim, emptying the first bottle of Kahlúa from his stash.

"You're nuts. If we get caught I'm going to tell them you've been trying to get me drunk since you sat down." Jana laughed, enjoying every sip of her doctored coffee. "That was great; do you want me to ask for another cup?"

"Sure, it looks like we're going to be here for a while as they're still loading luggage. That's the disadvantage of being the first to board, sure we get to enjoy a drink or two, have coffee, relax a little, but the wait is almost double of those having to wait in the terminal." He held up his hand, "I know, I know, it's better to be here than in the terminal, but it doesn't really feel better right now." He ran his hand through his hair, a nervous reaction, but he couldn't help it. He rose and went to the front of the plane, leaned over and whispered to the flight attendant, and then went to the bathroom.

Within seconds, the attendant brought fresh coffee. "Your son is so nice; it must be great to travel with him."

"He's nice to travel with, but he's not my son," she winked at the young woman with legs up to her neck. "I use and abuse them, and then let young women like you take them off my hands. Are you interested?"

"Well, maybe, but I-I don't think he'd be interested," she stammered not believing what she was being asked.

"He's a man, right?"

"Yes, ma'am, he's definitely a man." She blushed, excusing herself with haste, "I have other passengers to get settled." She walked away talking to herself.

As Charlie took his seat, he opened another small bottle and topped off their coffee. "So, do you still think this is a bad idea?"

"I never thought it was a *bad* idea, I just don't want to take the heat if you get caught. Oh and by the way, I think I got you a date once we land with that young flight attendant, the one with the killer legs."

"You did what?"

"She told me how nice it was to see me traveling with my son. Trust me; I'm *not* happy that a woman would think that would be the only way an older woman and younger man would travel together. So I told her I use and abuse young men and then turn them loose for others to reap the benefits of my training." She looked at Charlie, realizing he was speechless, his mouth was hanging open.

"You know I'm reconsidering whether you should be a cougar or not. This is making you crazy. Besides that, I don't need a date, and if I did I'd make my own arrangements." Looking aft his eyes fell on the taut skirt stretched tightly across the flight attendant's derriere, and he smiled to himself. *She is a pretty young thing and would definitely be a nice diversion for a couple of days. I'll definitely see what I can arrange.*

"Can I get you anything else before we take off?" the attendant asked Charlie when she returned.

Charlie leaned over and whispered in her ear. "Will you please bring my friend and I each a diet coke; what's your name?"

"I'll get that for you immediately," she whispered back. She leaned forward even more, thrusting out her breasts and the name tag, 'Anna'. Her pink tongue flicked at her pert lips, "I'm Anna." She walked down the aisle, swaying her hips just a little more pronounced for Charlie's visual pleasure.

"You're such a schmuck," Jana punched Charlie's arm.

"I'm just passing time. Besides, you wanted to set me up; why can't I put something together if I can? Oh, and by the way, why are we going to Frankfurt versus London? I thought our meetings were in London."

"They are Charlie, but our first meeting isn't until Monday afternoon and I really like Germany. I didn't think you'd mind. If you don't want to hang out with me, we can meet up on Monday morning for our flight to London."

"That sounds great. Do we have reservations in Frankfurt for the weekend?

"Yes, they're made, but you don't have to use them if you make other plans."

"I'll let you know after we arrive." He finished his drink and let the flight attendant know she could take the glasses when she had a chance. Reclining in his seat, he closed his eyes.

Jana relaxed in her seat as well, taking out a novel she'd picked up in the airport. She tried to read but her mind wouldn't focus. She closed her eyes and laid her head back. *Mike, how I wish you were here with me. The times we spent together this past week were ones I won't forget; definitely a high point in my life. The low point of course was the news about Craig. Damn, cancer. There are going to be some rough roads ahead. Liza will help.* She dozed off.

"Jana, wake up, we've been in the air about thirty minutes and I need a drinking partner."

Groggily she opened her eyes and smiled. "What are we drinking now?"

"I have some vodka and some more Kahlúa. Name your poison."

"I'll take the Kahlúa. It's the only alcohol I drink that is good in milk, soda or coffee. It's one you can drink with breakfast, lunch and dinner."

"I knew there was a reason I like this stuff too. You trained me well."

"Stop, just use your boyish charm and get us another soda we can share. What's for dinner, have you looked at the menu?"

"They have a fish; I think Salmon, and they have filet mignon both with vegetables and small potatoes. Anna said they'd be serving in a while." He looked at her, "What do you want to talk about?"

"Anna? Making good time, aren't you? Talk, anything you want, what's up with you?"

"I guess now's the time to tell you I can't sleep on an airplane."

"Actually you should have told me before we made the plans; I wouldn't have brought you."

"Don't be mad," he smiled, "I've never been able to relax enough to sleep. It used to make Sami crazy when I traveled with her."

"How is your mom anyway? Is she back from her honeymoon? Did she have a good time? Has she said anything about Mike?"

"I got a call from her yesterday and she and David are back and all settled. She wasn't going in to the office until Monday so she hadn't seen Mike yet. I think she was glad to be back though, not sure she really likes traveling so much anymore."

"I'm glad she's happy; she deserves it," Jana said

"Hey, "Charlie said, "it looks like they're getting ready to serve dinner. Are you hungry?"

"Starved, what are you doing?" Jana watched Charlie get up from his seat.

"See that young man, in the front row by himself."

"Yes, I see him so what?"

"Well he's traveling to Germany, alone, to report to an Air Force Base there. He seems like he could use someone to talk to. I'd like to suggest he come back and have dinner with you while I try to get some action going with Anna. Do you mind?"

"I don't mind," Jana studied the young man ahead of her, "his name is Marshal. We met while we were boarding the plane. If he's willing I'm game."

Charlie proceeded down the aisle and took the seat next to Marshal.

Jana watched as Marshal kept turning and smiling shyly at her as Charlie talked. *I shudder to think what he's telling that young man.* Opening her novel, she again tried to read. She noticed a movement to her left and looked up to see Marshal sliding into the seat. She welcomed him with her most alluring smile. "What did Charlie tell you to get you to change seats?"

"He said you were his boss and all you wanted to talk about was work. He asked me to come back here and see if I could distract you from the job for a while. You don't mind do you?" He flashed his most charming smile. "I think he really wants to see if he can score with Anna."

"I think your last assessment is probably right on the mark," Jana smiled, "but I don't mind at all. It will be nice to have a conversation with someone whose hormones aren't in overdrive."

"Who said my hormones weren't in overdrive? Don't get me wrong here, but I need to be totally honest; you're the most beautiful woman I've seen in a long time and I'd love to get to know you better."

"Really," she blushed.

"Yes," he glanced at the watch on his muscled forearm, "we have exactly eight hours to make that happen." He leaned over and kissed her softly on the lips.

"Young man, you're moving a little fast don't you think?"

"Actually, no, I don't think so. Life is short, and this may be the only time we have together. I don't want to let this opportunity get away from me."

Jana licked her lips, tasting her impetuous friend, "Are you trying to seduce me?"

"Not yet, but it's definitely something we can work on after dinner." He smiled taking her hand in his, lifting it to his mouth and kissing her palm, touching it ever so slightly with his tongue.

Jana shuddered; this could be one of the best flights across the pond she'd ever experienced. Gazing at Marshal, she smiled seductively, her non-verbal acquiescence to his plans, whatever they were going to be. Dinner was excellent, for airline food, and Jana was stuffed. "I can't eat another bite."

"I'm still hungry," Marshal said. "I'm going to see if they have any crackers." He rose and headed toward the galley.

I can't believe he's still hungry. I guess he's a growing boy.

Walking back to his seat Marshal smiled as he showed her two bags of chips. "Anna said she'd be serving a snack in another hour or so, but if I couldn't wait she'd serve me mine now. I told her these would carry me over until then. Do you want some?"

"No, I'm fine. Where do you put all that food? Do you have hollow legs or something?"

"No," his eyes twinkled, "nothing hollow on this frame anywhere," he smiled suggestively.

"Listen you need to stop that. We're on a plane, over the ocean. Your seat cushion also serves as a flotation device-*remember*?"

"Your point is," he whispered.

"Marshal, nothing is going to happen here. We're on an airplane for God's sake."

"True, but have you never heard of the mile high club?"

"I've heard of it," her eyes narrowed, "but I thought they were lying. I thought all those stores were exaggerations." She waved her hand, "I can't believe we're discussing this." The overhead lights were dimmed for those passengers who wanted to sleep.

Four

"*They certainly* make it convenient." Marshal lifted the blanket he was given and covered both of them, pulling her into his arms and laying her head on his shoulder. He kissed her softly as she snuggled closer. Marshal began to rub her arm slowly. He let his hand slip up under her blouse and pressed her breast, finding her flesh soft and warm.

"Have you lost your mind? We can't do this here," Jana pushed his hand away.

"Yes we can, just relax and enjoy yourself. I won't take you any further than you're willing to go. We're both consenting adults and I want to touch you. Feel what you do to me," taking her hand he laid it on his erection. "I want you Jana, now, here."

"We can't Marshal; there are people sitting all around us, they'd hear us."

"Does that mean you would if we weren't on this plane?"

"Well, no, I mean yes, I would…I think."

"Just lay back and relax. Follow my lead, okay?"

"Sure," she stuttered, "I—I can do that." Realizing her hand still rested on his erection, Jana began to rub it gently.

"You're not making this any easier," he whispered in her ear, kissing her and softly nibbling on her neck.

Jana felt Marshal's hand ease up her skirt. He fondled her

slowly, easing his hand up her leg and between her thighs. She parted her legs and Marshal moved his fingers to her core, easing two fingers into her nether region. Jana moaned softly.

"Just relax, take it slow, we have a lot of time to enjoy this," Marshal softly pressed his tongue into Jana's mouth. Their tongues entered a battle of wills, both wanting to control and yet wanting to submit to the ecstasy of the moment. As he pulled back, Marshal's hand traced the length of her legs as he removed Jana's panties.

"Marshal, give those to me."

"Later," he teased, "maybe, for now I want to keep them." He brought them up to his face, sniffed longingly, smiled, and stuffed them in his pocket.

"What? You're collecting women's panties?" she whispered. *She thought back to Mike, this must be a young man's new fetish, stealing underpants.*

"What do you think; this is some type of bed notching or something?" Marshal responded in his best western drawl.

She laughed.

Echoing her laugh, Marshal reached over and pulled her slowly to his side, kissing her once again. He covered them with the blanket as his hands immediately began to roam her body. "You're so beautiful. I just want to touch you everywhere."

"We can't. I don't want to be arrested by the German Polizei because of indecent exposure when we land."

"You won't, I just want to hold you and touch you. Let me Jana, please."

"I won't stop you," she said. "I seem to need your touch."

Marshal unbuttoned her blouse, opening her front hook bra. He took her breast in his strong hand and rubbed her nipple between his thumb and forefinger. She had a beautiful body and he desperately needed to make love to her. *How? I read where it's been done in the bathroom on the plane, I'm sure there's enough space.* Mike buttoned Jana's blouse and folded up the blanket.

"What are you doing?"

"I've got to go to the bathroom, come with me."

"I don't have to go to the bathroom." Her eyes questioned him.

"I don't either, but we can be alone in there." He placed her hand delicately on his crotch. "Feel this Jana, I'm hurting. Please come with me." Hand in hand they tip toed down the aisle.

Anna and Charlie watched the two enter the bathroom and the 'in use' sign illuminate. They smiled knowing exactly what was happening.

"We don't have a lot of time here." Marshal unbuttoned her blouse, leaning down he took one breast in his mouth and began caressing the other.

Jana reached down and unbuckled his belt, unzipping his pants. She backed up to the sink and Marshal lifted her wrapping her legs around his waist as he entered her in one easy stroke.

"Oh, Jana, I've died and gone to heaven." He moved in and out, kissing her neck, running his tongue along her shoulder. He lowered his head, concentrating on each and every move, faster and faster, feeling her body contract around him. Marshal pushed her up to the wall pressing into her again and again.

At the same time Jana's tongue assaulted his, moving in and out of his mouth in sync with his sexual moves. Jana ran her hands up under his shirt, rubbing his nipples, twisting and pinching them.

He moaned and pressed into her even harder and faster. He felt her sex contract around his cock as their orgasm peaked. Slowly Marshal sat down on the lid to the commode with Jana still riding his manhood. "I need a minute, but we're not done here…just, just give me a second to catch my breath."

With the words barely out of his mouth Jana felt his erection begin to grow again. *God I love the stamina of a young lover.* "I thought you said we didn't have a lot of time for this."

"Just once more, please," he begged. "Once wasn't enough to satisfy my need for you."

"Okay, once more," she laughed, "but you need to get your fill on this pass. We need to get out of this little room; the walls are closing in on me."

"Close your eyes and concentrate on satisfying yourself."

"What about your satisfaction?"

"Not to worry; I know if you're satisfied I'll be as well." Her toes were curling as she felt her second orgasm, or was it her third; begin to build in as many minutes as they had been together. Both sated, Marshal collapsed against her. "Marshal, we need to get *out* of this little room. You leave and give me a few minutes to get myself together. Oh," she held out her hand, "my panties."

"I'll leave, but I'm not ready to give you back your panties. If I did I'd just have to take them off again and why waste the effort." He laughed as he zipped his pants and buckled his belt. "Hurry, I'll be waiting." He kissed her nose as he opened the door and squeezed out.

Jana locked the door and looked at herself in the mirror. *Damn! I'm losing my mind. I've let someone I barely know make love to me twice, and on an airplane no less.* Reaching down, she took off her blouse and removed her bra. She put the blouse back on and tied it loosely at her waist with all the buttons open and her cleavage showing suggestively through the open front. She washed her female parts quickly, with cold water, hoping it would help to curtail the heat she felt; dried herself, straightened her skirt and opened the door. Her eyes immediately connected with Charlie and she blushed from head to toe. *He knows, damn it he knows. Shit!* She stood tall and walked to her seat noticing Marshal's stare, "What's the matter?"

"You took your bra off, didn't you?"

"Yes, you keep unfastening it so I figured I'd save the middle man, why?"

"I'm hurting again," he couldn't suppress the grin on his face, "can we go back to the bathroom?"

"No, we *can not*. I'm going to make you go sit with Charlie if you don't stop." She leaned over and kissed him, sucking his tongue through her teeth, curling his toes with her kiss. She heard him moan into her mouth as he pulled her close.

Jana closed her eyes enjoying their intimacy. "Marshal," she whispered, "tell me about you."

"Not much to tell. I'm on my way to Iraq. This is my last tour before I retire. I'm meeting a friend over there and we'll finish our careers together."

"You don't look old enough to retire, how old are you, if you don't mind me asking."

"I'm thirty-seven. I went in the Air Force when I was seventeen, spent time as an enlisted, got my degree and became an officer. I'm a Major and will retire at that rank. Though I've enjoyed being in the military, I've been to Iraq three times in the last three years and the odds aren't in my favor to come out in one piece. Being single I tend to do this a little more than the married guys. I've volunteered twice and I've hit the rotation once as well."

"So you'll retire while in Iraq?"

"No, they don't let you do that. I'll come back to the states, out process, and retire. Returning to the States is strictly a formality, I'll take some terminal leave and then retire. I've already begun looking for a job so I can make plans."

"What type of job are you looking for?"

"I work in Procurement; I'm a buyer for the troops. I've had a lot of training and believe I'd be a valuable asset to some of the big acquisition firms."

"That's what my son-in-law does as well. Do you know him?" She never even finished the question and Marshal answered.

"Yes, I know Jake."

Jana's eyes went wide; she'd had sex with one of her

son-in-law's colleagues. "You...know my son-in-law."

"Yes, I've known him for about seven years. In fact we went to school together both as officers and as procurement specialists."

Jana pulled back and studied his face, "Do I know you? Have we ever met?"

"No and yes; you don't know me, but we did meet at Jake and Liza's wedding."

"Oh my God, you're a friend of my son-in-law." Her eyes narrowed, "Was I set up here?"

"No, not-*exactly*; no one set you up."

"Not exactly! What the hell does that mean?" her whispers had a menacing quality, "Were Jake and Charlie involved in this?"

"Jana, keep it down you're attracting attention." He watched her take a deep breath. "In answer to your question, maybe a little, but it's no big deal, really."

"*Really?* You think not? Just tell me the truth."

"When Jake called me a couple of weeks ago and asked if I'd take the remainder of an assignment for one of his men, I said yes. When I talked to him day before yesterday he told me he got Liza a humanitarian move to live closer to her dad. He also mentioned that you and Charlie were leaving to go to Europe on business. I've known Charlie since the wedding as well so I called him. He gave me your flight information and I made my plans accordingly, hoping we could meet again." He saw the anger in her eyes, as her mouth tensed.

"Please, Jana, hear me out. I wanted to meet you. Jake and Charlie didn't do anything but give me information. They didn't know what I was planning, honestly. They knew when I met you at the wedding that I couldn't take my eyes off you. In fact they teased me about how infatuated I was with you. When Liza and Jake were married so were you. Jake told me later that you had gotten a divorce and even then I wanted to get to know you better, but he said the time wasn't right. So I've waited patiently. This flight, this time together, has been my doing. Please don't be mad at them, or me, for bringing us together. In fact both of them told me that the information they shared with me, your flight plans and such, were all they were willing to do. They wouldn't give me any additional help."

"Believe it or not Marshal, I'm flattered. To have waited what, three years to make this happen, I'm impressed." She opened her own blanket and leaned against the window, closing her eyes, pretending to sleep.

Marshal walked to the front of the plane, sitting in the empty seat next to Charlie. "I told her," he whispered, "and she wasn't exactly pleased; any suggestions?"

"Give her a little time. You've blown her away in more ways than one."

"But Charlie, I want to spend the weekend with her. I don't want her to hate me or to be mad at you, or Jake. You need to go and talk to her."

"Okay, I'll try, but if she's mad at you she's going to be furious with me." He reluctantly walked back to the seat next to Jana and sat down.

She turned slowly and eyed him suspiciously. "Returning to the scene of the crime are you?"

"It's not like that and you know it."

"Yea, I know." Leaning over she kissed him on the cheek. "Marshal's really nice and being with him has been-uh-interesting, certainly fun; so now what?"

"I'm going back up to work out arrangements for the weekend with Anna. I suggest I send Marshal back to you and the two of you do the same. Take the weekend to unwind with him, let the cougar within out and enjoy him thoroughly. We'll meet up on Monday morning at the airport and fly to London to do the work we came here to do. Are you game?"

"Yes, I'm game, but I have a question. Would I be out of line to offer Marshal a job when he gets out of the military? He'd be a great asset with his training. He could hit the ground running and would be available to start work about the time this new venture starts up. What do you think?"

"I think it'd be great. Just so you know, I think Jake was working on getting Craig to hire him so they could work together when they got out of the service. If you hire him first, it's just business."

"Yes, just business. Okay go send him back. He keeps turning and looking at us. I bet he's surprised I haven't pummeled you yet."

"I was worried about that too." Grinning from ear to ear, Charlie left to talk to Marshal. "Okay, you're clear. She forgives us. Oh, and by the way, she's going to offer you a job. I'd suggest you take it, as the fringe benefits would be fantastic."

Marshal sprang from the seat as if he was on fire. He tripped getting into the seat next to Jana.

"Back so soon?" she questioned

"I'm sorry Jana, really sorry. Everything else, us meeting before we boarded and our adventure in the bathroom was all my idea. I've wanted to make love to you since the day we met. You've been my fantasy for a long time, but I have to admit the real thing has been *so* much better."

"How about we sleep for a while?"

"Works for me; let me take the window and you can use me as your pillow." He smiled slyly.

"Okay, I'll try anything twice," getting up they exchanged seats and she slowly eased herself to his left with Marshal turning toward her. They were pressed tightly into each other.

Jana placed her head on his shoulder, slowly unbuttoning his shirt and running her hand up and down his chest. She played her fingers through the hairs on his chest, slowly encircling his nipples, twisting them slightly with each turn. Marshal shifted and Jana felt his erection build. "You need to take a cold shower," she whispered.

"I have a feeling this is going to be a permanent state for me as long as we're together." Lifting her chin, he savored a soft, seductive kiss. He reached his hand into her blouse taking her breast into his hand. "Woman, you're going to kill me."

Jana looked Marshal in the eye, smiled and slid slowly under the blanket, unzipping his pants and releasing his erection. She took him slowly into her mouth, rolling her tongue languorously over the head. She bobbed her head up and down over him. The things she did to his shaft with her tongue were incredible as she kept up a slight sucking pressure. Occasionally, she'd stop and rub the head with the palm of her hand while looking up into his eyes. She watched him grip the armrests as he let out a muffled groan and shot his load into her waiting mouth. Jana licked her lips as she slid back up to place her head on his shoulder.

Marshal covered them both, resting his hand on her breast. He realized her breathing had quieted. *Yes, I need sleep too my love*. He closed his eyes, wrapping his arms around her and resting his chin on the top of her head.

Five

Anna softly shook Jana's shoulder waking her. "We're going to be landing in about 45 minutes. Thought you might want some extra time to get ready. "

"Thanks Anna." Jana watched Marshal sleep; he was a handsome young man who was in desperate need of a shave. Jana reached down and pulled her carry-on out from under the seat. She rose, went to the bathroom, washed her face and brushed her teeth, putting fresh makeup on. She looked as good as it was going to get for now. As she stepped into fresh underwear she remembered Marshal had taken her panties and she needed to get them back. She left the bathroom and noticed Charlie sleeping soundly. *What a liar, he's going to pay for this several times this trip.*

She shook Marshal, waking him and leaning in to give him a kiss as she ran her hand along his jaw line. "You need a shave, but you do look rather rugged this way."

"Being in the military I don't get much of a chance to let it grow. Like most young men who leave the service, I intend to grow a full beard and mustache when I retire, one of my goals." He rubbed his hand across his jaw.

"Is that your only goal?"

"No, that's only one of my goals. My main one is to have a job lined up before I get out so I know where to set up home and such. I was going to try to do something completely different. You know venture out and try something I've never done before." He shook his head, as if to confirm this wasn't an option. "I decided my most saleable skill is exactly what I do today and I need to take advantage of it."

"You're right, it is, and working for an acquisition firm outside of the government is as different as night and day. That said, why don't you send me your resume and I'll see what I can do. The venture Charlie and I are working on will be in full testing at that time and we're going to need a person of your caliber to keep it all on track. If you're interested I'd like you to consider working for me."

"I'd like that very much, but are you sure; I mean after all we've slept together maybe working together isn't such a good idea. I do have another iron in the fire."

"I'm aware of your other iron and I'll match that offer and beat it. Sleeping with me will give you no advantages if you don't do the job I hired you to do." She watched him raise an eyebrow. "If I find you can't do the job, I'll personally show you the door, regardless of your prowess in the bedroom. Do we understand each other?"

Marshal eyes registered surprise at her directness. "Yes, but I have one other question."

"Okay, one more question and then we're done talking about work."

"What could I expect as a starting salary if I agreed to come to work for you?"

"Let's leave it like this. Whatever salary you can get Craig to offer you in writing," she laughed knowing Craig hated putting anything in writing, "yes, in writing, I'm willing to match and I'll raise by $10,000. So come and talk to me personally when you're ready."

He looked like the cat that ate the canary. "Ma'am, I'll do that."

"If you call me ma'am again the offer will be off the table forever," she laughed.

"Baby, I'll do anything you ask." He leaned over, kissing her softly on the cheek.

Jana pulled back from his scratchy face. "Then don't call me 'Baby' either. I'm not ma'am and I'm not your baby, do we understand each other?"

"Yes, I think we do. How about the weekend, do you want to come with me down to Kaiserslautern and spend the next two days seeing the local sights?"

"I'd like to spend the weekend with you, but I'd like to stay in Frankfurt and go to places around here. If you need to check in at the base we can go down and do that too, but I'd prefer to stay here. But you have to do something first."

"I don't have to report in until Monday, so staying here this weekend sounds fine to me. What about Charlie?"

"I think he's made arrangements with Anna, and if not he's on his own, he's old enough to find his own date. I still have something else you need to do for me."

"Yes, what's that?"

Laughing, Jana handed him a razor, "Shave please."

Marshal sprang from the seat and rushed to the bathroom. Within minutes he was back, clean shaven and refreshed. As the pilot came over the intercom advising the passengers that they had begun their descent into Frankfurt, Marshal took her hand in his. He smiled and whispered, "I'm glad you're not mad at us."

"I'm being purely selfish. I didn't want to give you up either. Don't wake me if I'm dreaming."

"Believe me you weren't dreaming. This has been the best flight of my life and I wouldn't change it for anything, well maybe I'd have made it last a little longer if I could have." He winked at her.

"You're incorrigible, do you realize that?"

"Insatiable maybe, but *very* corrigible; I hope I can satisfy my need for you this weekend. or it's going to be a long six months in Iraq." Marshal took her hand and intertwined her fingers with his.

*****

The plane landed and everyone began to rise and get their baggage together. Marshal took Charlie's bag out of the overhead and noticed he had done the same for him. Jana retrieved her items and stepped into the isle. She pressed back against Marshal, feeling him tremble as she deliberately rubbed her body against him.

"Behave yourself, or I won't be responsible." The line started moving and they began to exit the plane.

Once in the terminal Charlie caught up with Jana, "I'll meet you at the airport on Monday."

Jana watched Charlie walk away, hand-in-hand with Anna. "I guess it's just you and me." When Marshal didn't respond she looked at him, "Marshal, you don't have to stay with me if you have other plans. We had fun on the plane, it was great, but I don't want you to feel obligated to be with me."

"Lady, you really have this all wrong." He pulled her out of the surge of passengers moving through the terminal, turned her toward him and kissed her with unbridled passion. "Jana, I want to be with you. I've wanted to be with you for over three years. This weekend is a dream come true and I intend to take full advantage of the time we have together. The plane ride was the ultimate and the weekend will be my greatest fantasy come true. I want to be with you. I want to learn everything I can about you. But most of all I want to make love to you continuously for the next couple of days." Taking her hand he placed it once again on his erection. "Every time I think of you or remember what happened on the plane I get hard. We need to get our luggage, get through customs and get to a hotel as soon as possible, agree?" His eyes were pleading with her for agreement.

"Agree!" They headed for the passport control and baggage claim. Finally clearing customs, Jana watched Charlie getting into a waiting cab with Anna. He waved and smiled giving her a thumbs-up. Shaking her head she turned to Marshal. "I've got reservations at the Steigenberger, Hotel Frankfurter Hof."

"Sounds kind of up-scale, Jana, I don't have the type of clothes for a place like that. Are you sure we shouldn't stay somewhere else?"

"Yes, I'm sure, we'll be spending a lot of time in our room," she smiled. "We'll go down to the walk platz this afternoon and get you a nice shirt and tie you can wear to dinner tonight. I won't take no for an answer as you're my guest. Please, Marshal let me do this for you, it'll be fun. Then we can go straight to our room after dinner."

"Okay, but you need to let me pay for some of this."

"You can buy lunch. There's this little restaurant off the hotel called Oscar's. They have some great Hasenruckenfilet and their fried potatoes are to die for. I really love the fresh meats the Germans raise for their restaurants. I also like their salads and fresh vegetables." Her eyes lit up, "The beer isn't bad either, especially the Weizen beer. I have to tell you, before I visited Germany; I didn't drink beer or coffee. After spending some time here I learned how excellent both are. I used to have friends who visited here bring me coffee; now of course I can find it in some of the local specialty shops."

"You're kidding right? Beer is beer…coffee is coffee."

"I'll make you a bet, if by the end of this weekend you don't agree with me about the beer and the coffee; I'll give you a $5,000 signing bonus."

"What makes you think I'll be honest with that kind of offer sitting on the table?"

"Because I know you're an honest man and I know you won't lie to me. You've already proven that."

"How could you know that for sure, we only met a few hours ago?"

"Actually we've known each other for three years and with what's passed between us within the last few hours, I'm sure I have a pretty good idea how to make you tell me the truth." She leaned in pressing her hand against his groin.

"You don't play fair." He groaned taking her hand in his, bringing it to his lips. He opened her door to the cab and gave the driver their destination. Pulling from the curve Marshal looked her in the eye and smiled longingly. "How far away is the hotel?"

"Not far," she whispered brushing her lips across his.

*****

Entering their room, Jana threw her purse on the bed. "I need to take a shower and freshen up. I can't go to sleep, even though I'd like to, or I won't sleep tonight. Then we can go get something to eat. I'm really hungry, how about you?"

Marshal pulled her into his arms and kissed her neck, "I'm starved, but not for food."

"I'm going to take a bath, would you like to join me." Jana seductively removed her skirt and blouse and walked naked to the bathroom. *I need to get my panties back from this guy before I leave on Monday.*

"Be right with you," Marshal muttered as he quickly removed his clothes, leaving them in a heap on the floor. The bathroom was filling with steam as he pulled back the curtain, eand eyed Jana from head to toe. "Woman you are beautiful, you have the most voluptuous body I've ever seen." His hands cupped her breasts, kneading them, smiling as her nipples hardened in response. Leaning down he kissed one, then the other. He lowered his hand, slowly circling her lower abdomen, easing into her pubic hair, letting his fingers enter her slowly, first one, then two. He felt her muscles tighten around them. Spurred on by this encouragement he added another finger.

"Can I do something for you?" she murmured, her head fell back, her eyes closed.

"Jana, feel how hard I am," he guided her hand to his erection.

She wrapped her fingers around the girth, feeling it gain firmness with each caress.

They silently touched each other, until he simply had to be inside her. He placed her hands on his shoulders as he lifted her, positioning her, easing his erection into her inner passage. He caught his breath, pausing to savor her narrow entrance, but somehow she maneuvered herself to take him fully in a single stroke. The warm water cascaded over them and their sexual heat flared as she rode his magnificent cock. They reached their orgasms simultaneously, and he quickly felt her second orgasm begin, so he didn't slow his assault. Within minutes he felt her body tense again as another orgasm overtook her. He peaked, releasing himself into her, and taking her lips in an earth shattering kiss. He eased out slowly, realizing he was still erect, and entered her several more times with utter determination. She met him, stroke for stroke. He again lowered his head to take her nipples, first one and then the other, into his mouth, hearing her moan softly. Marshal knew she could go longer, but he needed a break. He gently lowered her to her feet. Taking the soap from the tray he began to wash her, concentrating on her breasts and swollen mound.

"I *think* those are clean," she grabbed the soap from him, "let me return the favor." Her soft, soapy hands massaged his cock and balls, the sensual ministrations making him collapse against the shower wall.

"I'm starting to prune up," she laughed as she stepped from the shower, "rinse yourself off lover boy." She dried herself, "I'm still hungry, actually more so if that's possible. Let's get dressed and go down to Oscar's."

"Works for me, I've definitely worked up an appetite. After lunch we can walk down to the walk platz and enjoy a beer and maybe desert. Sounds like we'll be spending the rest of the day eating, doesn't it?"

"Not only eating and drinking, I was promised sex on this adventure, and that better be a big part of your plans," she teased as she handed him a towel.

"Yes, sex, definitely—sex and more sex, as much as I can physically accommodate." He stroked her backside as he stepped around her making his way to his suitcase.

*****

Looking into the store window Jana found the perfect shirt for Marshal. It was a soft teal with a matching tie. It would be gorgeous with his dark hair and hazel eyes. Being a good foot taller than she was didn't hurt either. In fact he was perfect, broad shoulders, narrow hips and a willingness to please her insatiable appetite for sex. She couldn't have asked for a better plan for her weekend if she'd planned it herself. As she had suspected he looked fantastic in the shirt. Adding the tie only made him look more sophisticated. Jana eyed a beautiful green German jacket. *God, Marshal would look so good in this*. She nodded to the clerk and immediately the right size appeared. "Try it on Marshal; I want to see it on you."

"Jana, I don't need a jacket."

"I know, but try it on anyway. Do you like the teal shirt, or would you like a different color?"

"Truthfully, I'd like something in a more neutral color. I would really like to think I'd wear it more than once, but I can guarantee you I wouldn't with the teal."

"Understand," Jana nodded, "Do you have this in a soft yellow, beige, or blue color?" The clerked confirmed she did and Jana indicated she'd take one in each of those colors as well as the teal. “Can you have it delivered to the Steigenberger, Hotel Frankfurter Hof this afternoon?” The clerk assured she’d take care of it personally, and Jana and Marshal left the store in search of a beer at one of the outside cafes.

“You had all those shirts and the jacket sent to the room didn’t you?”

“Yes, I did.” The waiter approached and Jana ordered them each a Wiezen beer and apple strudel.

“I didn’t need four shirts or a jacket.”

“Need had nothing to do with the buy Marshal. I bought those things for you for two reasons; one I can, and two, because I wanted to. You look good in them; I couldn’t pass them up. Besides, you’ll be able to wear all of them when you come to work for me. You’re not always going to be in the military you know.”

“True, but in the meantime I’m going to have to carry all this extra stuff all over the globe.”

“Four shirts and a jacket don’t weigh much. I think a big strong man like you can handle it. But if it’s a problem, I’ll have them sent back to my place in the States on Monday morning and you can pick them up when you come there to work. How does that sound?”

“I guess that’s also an option. Not a bad one all things considered.” He held up his beer, “You think of everything.” He smiled as he took a drink, “This is really good.” *Jana’s right, this beer is a lot better than the Budweiser or Miller at my dad’s place.*

Six

Jana felt her cell phone vibrate, *It's Liza; I wonder what's going on.* She noted the time difference made it ten in the morning back home. "Liza, what's up?"

"Mom there's something going on with dad," Liza blurted.

"What do you mean, something going on? What are you talking about?"

"Mom, dad came back from the doctor this morning, walked to his liquor cabinet, took out a bottle of Scotch and went and sat on the patio. He's been drinking for over an hour-and he won't talk to me."

Jana was concerned, even for Craig this was strange behavior. "Has he said anything at all? Have you tried to talk to him?"

"Yes, mom. I've asked him repeatedly what happened at the doctor's office, but the only thing he says is 'I've got to get my affairs in order' and then he takes another drink. Do you have any idea what is happening here? Hell, mom you were married to the man forever."

This wasn't good. *He got bad news about his cancer. Shit!* "Liza, put your dad on the phone."

"Why?"

"Do you want me to find out what's going on, or do you

just want to guess?" Jana was losing patience with her daughter. She listened as Liza handed Craig the phone and told him it was Jana.

"Jana, is it really you?" Craig asked hesitantly.

"Yes, Craig; how are you doing?" She was already aware there was a serious problem, but tried to remain calm.

"I'm fine, went to the doctor this morning."

"Craig, what did the doctor tell you? Weren't you supposed to get the test results this morning?"

"Yes, I did."

His terse answers created a tension over the connection. "Craig, damn it, tell me what the doctor told you."

"He told me to get my affairs in order."

"That's all he said? Craig there had to be more than that; I want the details. What did the doctor tell you?"

"Jana, will you marry me?"

"No, Craig, I won't. Now tell me what the doctor told you."

"I told you."

"Craig, you're pissing me off. What did the doctor say? Do I have to call him myself to find out?" Her voice was rising, and she realized not only did she have Marshal's undivided attention, but other guests at the outside café were watching as well.

"I don't have prostate cancer."

"That's good, isn't it?"

"Actually no, it's not. I have pancreatic cancer-and Jana-it's spread to my liver. The doctor gives me maybe a month."

"But what about treatment? Surely there's something that can be done." She heard the desperation in her voice.

"Not really, the doctor said that it's too advanced to do surgery, and that chemotherapy would not help at this stage."

"Oh Craig, I'm so sorry. Is Liza standing there?"

"No, she ran in the house after my last comment." He felt bad, but he was the one dying, not her. "I know I should have told her in some other way, but I didn't know how. Crap, Jana, I'm a mess."

"Craig, I understand, do you need me to come home?"

"No, finish your trip. You coming back won't change what's going on here. I'll talk to Liza." He looked up as his daughter approached.

"Craig, you need to stop drinking, you're scaring her."

Craig knew she was right, but he didn't know what to do any more. As Liza approached he asked her, "Do you want to talk to your mom? Jana she wants to talk to you. Don't worry we'll work this out when you get back." He hesitated a moment before giving the phone to Liza, "Jana don't worry; I'm fine-under the circumstance." He gave the phone to Liza.

"Mom, what should I do?"

"Nothing, you can't fix this. Let him wallow in his Scotch bottle for a while. He'll snap out of it. You're dad's strong; he'll do what he needs to do, once he realizes he's the one who owns this process from here on out."

"Mom, I'm scared."

"Me too, baby, but we both have to be strong for your dad. Give him a big hug and kiss for me and I'll see you soon. Liza if you need to talk, call me any time, okay?"

"Okay mom, I love you."

"I love you too. Liza, you need to get in touch with Jake. Let him know what's happening, he might have some ideas for you."

"I will mom, talk to you soon."

Jana closed her cell phone and her eyes, tears sliding down her cheeks. *He's dying, I never expected this*.

Marshal moved closer taking her in his arms, "Everything will be fine, Jana. Remember God never gives us more than we can handle."

"Thanks, I think. I'm worried about Craig, but I'm also concerned about Liza. As mad as she gets at her dad she loves him unconditionally. This is going to be rough on her and Jake's not there to help her through this. Knowing the military, they won't send him home until Craig dies; am I right?"

"Pretty much, with Jake in Iraq, it will be hard to get him out of there any sooner than his rotation dictates."

"I was going to suggest we go back to the room, but I think I'd like to get drunk."

"Okay, we can do it here, or we can go to the room and order room service."

"Let's stay here for a little while. I enjoy watching the people. Believe it or not I think it helps." She laughed softly but the laughter didn't reach her eyes.

Marshal had to do something, maybe talking about her ex-husband would help. "Tell me about him Jana. What is Craig like? What was your marriage like?"

Jana laughed softly as she remembered the craziness of their marriage, this time her laughter reached her eyes and the tears once again flowed. "Sorry!" she apologized. "Marriage to Craig was interesting. We always seemed to be striving to achieve something from the day we were married. He's a muscian, did you know that? No, probably not. Anyway he played in rock and roll bands when we first got married; that's what we lived on. He was good, really good." She smiled softly as she remembered. "We were poor as church mice but we were happy." She stopped talking as her memories continued.

Marshal encouraged her to finish, "Then what, he doesn't play now, does he?"

"No, he plays guitar now more than drums, but he still has those drums, and a lot of guitars, maybe twenty?" *What are we going to do with those?*

"When we went into business together it was a nightmare. He didn't like giving up any of the control of the company to me. He was boss; you know 'I am man and thus boss' issue. Well I wouldn't stand for it. I wanted equality and as our culture moved in that direction Craig was made to do the same thing, even though he resisted for a long time. He knew I was smart, and valued my opinion on the direction we were taking the business, but I can tell you I sat in plently of meetings where I was not even recognized as an employee, let alone a partner."

Marshal shook his head, "Wow, you've come a long way if that's how your company started."

"No it wasn't like that. It wasn't like one day everything changed—it just did. The world changed and Craig did too. We grew up together with the company and that was great for both of us."

"I hate to ask this question, but why did you get a divorce if it was as you say."

"It wasn't always good, in the end it was just a job and it wasn't very enjoyable. We just stopped working at our marriage and finally realized we weren't moving forward anymore, at least not together. So we decided, very amiably I might add, that we'd be better apart. We've stayed friends, we still fight, and we both love our daughter, but I know the divorce was the only option we had."

Marshal noticed her beer was empty, "Do you want another beer?"

"Yes, thanks. One more and then we'll head back to the hotel."

"Jana, are you okay?"

"Yes, I suppose as good as can be expected. I really don't have much choice here, do I?" She looked at him hard, "Marshal, if you'd like to go to the base I understand. I'm probably not the best company right now."

"I'm not going anywhere Jana. I'm in this for the long haul. If you want we can talk; I'll hold you; I'll make love to you; but most of all I'm here for you."

She reached over and sqeezed his hand. "Thanks, Marshal, I'm glad you're here. I really need a friend right now."

Marshal ordered them both another beer as well as a bratwurst they could share. He figured he'd better get some food in her along with all the alcohol.

Seven

The rest of the weekend passed quickly, although the sexual excitement had been diminished by the family crisis. Jana and Marshal made love, and he held her while she cried over the problems she knew she'd face when she got home. Liza hadn't called, which surprised her. Now though, she had work to do, and a flight to catch. Marshal shared a cab to the airport with her and reluctantly left to catch a bus to the base. He said he'd stay in touch, and she knew she could always find out how he was from Liza or Jake. She smiled, *I guess the cougar is alive and well.* As she finished checking in and moving to her gate she noticed Charlie sitting alone at a table. "You look like you lost your last friend. Care if I join you?"

"Please," he stood and pulled out an empty chair, "no, I'm fine, I was just thinking that's all."

"About what?"

"You, Sami, the cougar lifestyle, as well as your in-flight adventure."

She ordered coffee, "What brought this on?"

"I just want the women in my life to be happy."

"Believe me, we're very happy."

"Maybe I'm worried about what will happen with all the problems you'll face when we get home."

"What are you talking about?" *I haven't said anything to*

him, does he know? “Is there something I’ve missed here?”

“Marshal called me and gave me a heads up about Craig. I’m concerned about how manipulative he can be when he wants you to do something for him.”

“Don’t be, that’s exactly why I asked Liza to come home. She will help me work through all this with her dad. Tell you what; let’s not worry about this now. They’re boarding our flight for London and we have some things to go over before we arrive.” She finished her coffee, “Let’s focus, time to get back to work.”

Jana settled into her first-class seat. The problem with Craig was going to impact her there was no way it wouldn’t. A man she’d loved, a man who was the father of her daughter, was dying and there was nothing she could do. As she closed her eyes and took another deep breath to steady her nerves, she knew she had to concentrate on her current business venture. There were issues that needed to be worked, but nothing she couldn’t handle. *Still, I have a lot of crap on my plate right now.* Jana went over their agenda for the day and her plan for getting exactly what she wanted.

“Jana?”

“Yes, Charlie.”

“I love watching you work. You’re an amazing woman.”

“Thanks,” she lifted her coffee in a semi-toast, “to the venture and its success and to Charlie, for letting the cougar out of her cage.”

*****

As they departed the flight Charlie assisted Jana with her carry on. “Why didn’t you check this one too?”

“Because it has my jewelry in it, and checking it is not a good idea. I tend to lose things that way.”

“Just asking. Don’t worry; I got it, not a problem,” he mumbled.

"Charlie, quit whining, it's not that heavy. I've been toting that case for over twenty years. Sometimes you're such a baby."

"Stop with the baby jokes, I said I have it. Is there a car meeting us once we clear customs?"

"Yes, there'll be a car so we should make the meeting without a problem."

"Jana, if we get done today, are we going to try to catch a flight tonight?"

"Yes, that's my plan; we have reservations on three different flights this evening with a fall back tomorrow if we don't complete our business today. I'm hoping we finish up this morning so we can sneak out and get some fish and chips at a nice pub before we leave town. Are you game?"

"Sure sounds great. Exactly why am I along on this trip Jana, just curious?"

"Actually I thought it'd be good for you to put some faces and names together since you'll be coordinating my activities with these people. That said, I also think if you find you can handle this, when I'm busy I could send you over here alone to handle things for me. At times I think you know as much about this venture as I do."

"You really think I could do this without you?"

"Sure, and I need someone to be *my* voice and not their own. By bringing you along I've indicated my confidence in you. If you have to come back on your own they'll provide you the same respect."

"Sounds like a plan. I thought you were just giving me a bonus by letting me tag along. Yes, I pay attention and I know the details of this merger. Do you want me to handle some of this for you?"

"No, not this trip, these guys are use to working with Craig. They need to understand that *I'm in charge* of my company and I make the decisions. Once that's established I could send Mickey Mouse over here and they would trust that I knew what I was doing. They need to trust me first. Then you can step in and finish up the details. Did you ever see the movie *Pretty Woman*?" Seeing Charlie's face she began to laugh.

"Sure I've seen it a couple of times. Don't laugh I know it's a chick flick but Julia Roberts is hot."

"Do you remember where Richard Gere decides how his business is going to be handled and makes the decision to move forward, then he leaves it up to his people to settle the merger, well that's what I'll do today. I'll settle the merger, assuming I like the final plan, and then I'll tell the group that you will close the deal while I make some phone calls. That establishes your position in my company. Are you ready to do this?"

"Sure, between you and my mom you've been training me to take this on since I started working. I'm ready Jana, really. This will be great." *I'm excited I can't believe she's going to let me do this.*

They cleared customs and met their car and driver. When they entered the building lobby a young woman welcomed them and led them to the conference room. "Hi, I'm Laura; I'll be your escort today. We're all excited to have you here," she smiled, shyly.

"It's good to meet you too, Laura, I'm Jana and this is Charlie. We're glad to be here."

"The meeting is in our main conference room. If you'll please follow me; I'll take you there."

"Sounds great, we're ready." On the walk to the conference room Laura talked continually about the business, the people who worked there, and the city that supported them.

Jana was surprised at the depth of the young woman's knowledge. "Where did you learn all that information, Laura?"

"My dad has worked here all his life and I've worked here since I got out of college. I guess you could say I grew up here. I love this company and all it stands for."

Jana stopped the woman in mid-stride, "Laura, what are you trying to tell me?"

"Please don't close us Ms Gates. We're a profitable, small company with strong work ethics and we'll make you proud to own us."

"Laura, let me be the first to guarantee you that I'm not here to close down this company. In fact, for your info, I'm actually hoping to broaden the business market for your goods to the American consumer. If we can make it work, the company will get bigger, not smaller. Okay?"

"Yes ma'am and thank you." Smiling from ear to ear, Laura opened the conference room door and escorted Jana and Charlie to her father. "Dad, this is Ms Gates and Mr. Brandon. Ms Gates, Mr. Brandon this is my father Dale Brown."

"Mr. Brown it's good to finally meet you. I know it's not your custom to call us by our first names but I'd be pleased if you called me Jana, and this is Charlie."

"You can call me Dale. I'll introduce you to the rest of my management team in a few minutes but first we need to know what your plans are-if you don't mind. We're curious and a little afraid."

"I'm sorry, Dale, if I'd known that was what was going on here I would have come sooner." Looking around the room, Jana motioned for everyone to take a seat. "Please make yourselves comfortable. First of all let me assure you I have no intention of closing down this company. As I told Laura, my goal is to make this company bigger, expanding your market to include the American consumer. I like the quality of your products and I think Americans will as well. Nothing will change in how you manage this company other than the fact that you might find you need to hire more people. I'll still want you to manage this company and I would also like to invite you and your management team to America to visit my offices. This will give them a chance to put faces with names as we move forward. I'll want you to work directly with Charlie if you need anything. Does anyone have any questions?"

A young woman, about Charlie's age stood up, "You say you don't plan to make any changes but how is that possible if you want to expand our market?"

"Good question, Charlie would you like to answer that for her?"

"Yes, ma'am; we don't want to put any additional machine runs into operation until we're sure we have the customer base in America. Through analyses of your floor space and your machine lines, we feel we can start up one additional production line within 60 days. Once we finish the product testing we'll know how soon we have to start the second line. So for now, we'll leave everything as it is and make any changes we need to make slowly. If a decision is made to expand we'll need some time to meet with you and figure out how we proceed. Does that answer your question?"

"Yes, thank you," taking her seat she smiled.

Jana opened a leather binder, "If we can take some time to review the agreement..."

"Are there any other questions?" No one else said anything. "With no further questions, all that has to be done is to get a few signatures and we can consider our merger complete." Everyone clapped excitedly. "I'll sign this document and leave it to Charlie to finish things up. If you'll excuse me I need to call my daughter. Thanks again to all of you for your time." Jana left the room and realized that Laura was immediately by her side.

"Ms Jana, let me take you to my father's office so you have privacy for your call."

"Thank you, Laura, that's very kind." Jana dialed Liza's cell. It rang once, twice, three times and then went to voice mail. *Where is she?* Jana dialed her home phone and again it rang once, twice, three times and no answer. *Where could she be, it's only 6:00 a.m. and she's normally not an early riser. On second thought let me try Craig's office.* On the second ring, Liza answered.

"Hello parental unit, how's your trip going?"

"Liza, you worried me to death. I called your cell and the condo and there was no answer."

"Sorry mom, forgot to turn the cell back on after I left the hospital yesterday. They hospitalized dad to run some test and to give him some mega vitamins. He's still there; I'll spring him this afternoon. He's doing as good as can be expected. So again, how's your trip going?"

"It's going better than I thought it would. Once I told them I had no plan to close their operation, they've been very supportive. We will finish up within the hour and be on a plane this afternoon. I should be back late tomorrow. You said your dad was getting some kind of treatment; I thought they couldn't do anything for him?"

"They can't. I talked to his doctor and basically they're feeding him intraveniously because he's not eating enough. That's one of the side effects of the cancer, he just can't eat."

"Liza, does dad know about this?"

"Not exactly, the doctor asked me and I said do it. I don't want to lose him mom."

Jana heard her crying. "Liza you need to stop this. Your dad will be furious if he learns you're keeping him alive. He's not a dog, Liza, he's a person and he'd hate this. This is the last time you do this, do you agree?"

"Yes mom." She sniffed, "I knew you'd be mad, but mom I didn't want him to die before you got back."

"Don't be silly, knowing your dad like I do he's going to wait until I can be there so I'm miserable too. Aren't you in the office early?"

"Actually Charlie called me this morning and asked me to send over some documents he needed to provide to Dale Brown. He also wanted the last pages of the merger document changed to include three signatures on our side and six on the side of the merged company. Not sure why he needed that but I took care of it and he should have it by now. I'm glad everything is going the way you want. I'll be glad when you're here. I really don't want to do this by myself. I've got about twenty questions for you. I'd ask dad but he's resting and I think that's more important right now."

"Is there anything you need me to answer right now?"

"No, I've got it under control. I've made some decisions already I think you need to do a sanity check on for me, but everything else can wait. How was your flight over there?"

"I'm confident you've done a good job but I'll be glad to take a look if it will make you feel good. The flight over was nice-in fact I met someone Jake knows."

"Who's that?"

"His name was Marshal, said he was at your wedding, though I don't remember him."

"You mean Marshal Upton. Yes, he was at the wedding. Jake and Marshal went through Staff Officer School together and have stayed in touch. In fact, Jake did tell me Marshal was meeting up with him in Iraq; he gets out of the service the same time Jake does. They both retire when they return from Iraq. You might want to look at hiring him. I think in some ways he has better qualifications than Jake, but don't tell him I told you that," she laughed.

"Yes we had a long talk on the flight and I did tell him to contact me when he got out of the service and we'd hook him up. He doesn't look old enough to retire though."

There was a pause on Liza's end, and then she spoke, "Tell me if I'm out of line here, okay. Just how well did you get to know Marshal? Jake said if he didn't know better he'd say Marshal was smitten with you."

"Smitten?" Jana laughed.

"Yea, that's what he said, the exact word. Is there something I need to know here?"

"No, Liza there's nothing you need to know. Both

Marshal and I are consenting adults and we enjoyed each other's company while I was in Germany."

"Moooommmm! Damn, he's a friend of Jake's. Why would you do this?"

"Liza, take your puritanical attitude and keep it to yourself. I'm only going to say this one more time. Both Marshal and I are consenting adults. Leave it alone."

"Okay mom, jeez, I can't believe you. You're right you two can do whatever you want. I question the adult factor, but it is what it is. You make this an uncomfortable situation for Jake and me. Hell, I may need therapy."

"Only in your mind Liza. If you talk to Jake he's going to tell you to mind your own business and that's *my* suggestion as well. Do you need me for anything else, if not I've got to cut this off so Charlie and I can catch our flight."

"Have a good flight home, but please behave yourself, or at least try," she laughed. "I love you mom, see you soon."

Eight

Boarding yet another plane, Jana was pumped. Her new international corporate acquisition couldn't have gone better. It was run by a dedicated group of managers and Dale Brown and his daughter were priceless. Looking over the contract she was pleased with her success, "Charlie."

"Yes."

"Young man you are amazing. You did your homework and made sure they were comfortable. You also knew he preferred working with a man-didn't you."

"That used to be true. Laura and I had a chance to talk for a few minutes as she walked me to meet you. She said her dad always felt a woman's place was in the home, but since she joined the company he's decided woman are an important element, especially when his products deal with the female consumer. Dale attended a class recently where he was shocked to find more women shopped on the internet than men and that they bought their husbands clothes. Laura said her and her mom let him in on a little secret as well."

"What's that?"

"That they'd been buying his clothes for years and giving them to him on his birthday and Christmas because they knew he wouldn't return them or not wear them. Basically he'd been wearing what they wanted him to wear all his life," Charlie laughed.

"It's the truth you know. I remember when Craig and I were first married. His secretary told me once she knew when I was traveling because she was convinced he was fashioned impaired. I got so I put a tie and shirt together for him as well as pants so he'd look good when I was gone. I wish I'd thought about those clothes for kids where symbols match the pants and the tops. They need to do that for husbands, it'd be so much easier."

"I don't have that problem. I know more about fashion than most women. It has a lot to do with Sami-and a lot to do with you. Don't tell anybody," he whispered. "I do love to go shopping for clothes."

"You're a kick Charlie. I've know you love to shop almost as much as I do."

"Not funny. I'm tired, how about you."

"I'm exhausted, but it's a good feeling." She leaned back and closed her eyes.

Charlie felt her relax and noticed the soft rise and fall of her chest. Yes, rest was exactly what the cougar needed. Smiling, he too leaned back and closed his eyes. The flight took off without either one of them noticing.

Charlie stirred in his seat. "I can't believe we slept through most of the flight. I'm starving."

"Me too, we'll get something to eat when we clear customs."

"I don't think I can wait that long."

"Then ask the flight attendant for something."

"Okay, do you want something?"

"Just bring me whatever you get, and I'd like something to drink, but need to use the restroom first." Jana walked down the aisle. As she entered the restroom she smiled, *I remember a much better use of this facility on the flight over the pond.*

*****

Clearing customs was a nightmare. *You'd think the feds could get this worked into a more streamlined process. No, it's as it always is when dealing with a large bureaucracy, hurry up and wait. I can't understand the rationale of asking the same questions to someone gone a week and someone gone a year. Damn, just hurry up for God's sake.*

As Jana approached the customs counter she was ready to scream. She spent the next ten minutes answering questions. 'Were you on a farm; did you bring in any vegetables or meats into this country; how long were you out of the country; where did you travel to; was it business or pleasure; do you have anything to declare?' It was more like a survey. *I wonder it I told them I had a suitcase full of contraband would the agent even pause or just type yes in the on-line questionaire he seemed to be filling out as he asked his questions. He reminds me of a dedicated gossip monger obtaining fodder for his morning coffee break.* Convinced it didn't really matter, Jana answered each and every question knowing she wouldn't clear this point without crossing the t's and dotting the i's. *What a bloody joke.*

*****

In the back seat of the company car, Jana heaved a sigh of relief. *As much as I love going to Europe it's a major pain getting there and back.* "Charlie, you want us to drop you off at your apartment or do you want to go into the office?"

"I'll go to the office with you. I have some things I need to take care of and my car is there."

"Steven, please take us to the office."

"Yes, ma'am."

"Jana, don't you want to go home; shower and change first?"

"No, I'll shower in my office. I have work to do as well. If you want you can take a shower there too."

"I might take you up on that, we'll see."

"I need you to set up a meeting with Cheryl, say in an hour or so. I want to know how she did on hiring the new managers. Then I need to go see Liza. I want to help her with the issues at the office and talk her through what's going to happen with Craig."

"Are you planning to go over and see him?"

"I wasn't planning on it, but if Liza wants me too, I will. There are a lot of things to work out if he only has a month left. Tomorrow should be soon enough to get into all that. To tell you the truth, I think it'll be best if I wait for Liza. It's so easy for me to slide back into that *wife mode* and I need to prevent that. I talked to Liza before we left England and she agrees. In fact, she told me if I did she was going to walk up behind me and smack me in the back of the head." She smiled, knowing that's exactly what her daughter would do too.

"If I were you I wouldn't give her the opportunity," Charlie laughed at the predicament she was in. "Don't worry, I'll protect you."

"From Liza? I seriously doubt it."

Jana's cell vibrated and she answered, "Yes Liza, what's up?—Sure you're taking your dad home and putting him to bed—Okay, I understand. I'll meet you at the condo in the morning—No, I'm fine. I wanted to meet with Cheryl; maybe I can get her to have dinner with me—You take care, love you sweetheart, see you tomorrow."

"I guess that's settled, you're having dinner with Cheryl?" Charlied questioned.

"Yes, if she's available, and quite frankly I think I could use the down time."

*****

"Cheryl thanks for joining me tonight. I didn't want to eat alone and I sure didn't feel like cooking."

"Not a problem, I don't think I've ever been here. Is this place new?"

"No, I think it's been here a while. Charlie and I have come here to lunch a couple of times and I've had dinner here as well. I like the decor, and the waiters are all college students, very cute."

"You're nuts. Speaking of college students, the rumor mill has you married to our lead accountant. Please tell me they're not talking about Sean."

Jana nearly spilled her pomegranate martini, "Let me set the record straight. No, I'm not getting married, and no I'm definitely *not* seeing Sean. Give me a break. However," she smiled shyly, "I did date Mike, our previous lead accountant, for an entire week."

Cheryl studied Jana, and ventured further, "In my wildest dreams I couldn't imagine dating a man that age. In fact, I'm pretty sure I have shoes older than he is." Cheryl raised her hand to the waiter indicating they needed another round of drinks. "You're amazing Jana. How'd you decide on this course of action, a younger man? I'm going to make you my mentor if you can tell me how I can get some of that action. We could start a club or something. What do you think?"

"Cheryl, you're crazy. Okay, okay to be in my club you have to answer a single question."

"Question, I can do that, what type of question?"

"No, I'm not giving you any hints. It's like this, if you answer my question correctly, I'll tell you everything I know. If you can't answer it, you're on your own." Jana raised her hand, beckoning the waiter for another round of drinks.

The waiter quickly arrived with their drinks, "Ladies, how about something to eat?"

"We'll get to that eventually," Jana responded with a sexy smile.

"Okay how about an appetizer? My treat," he added.

"No, not yet, maybe later." Jana looked into the young man's beautiful green eyes, "Don't worry about us. We're not driving, so we can drink as much as we want. In fact," reaching into her purse Jana took out a business card, handing it to the waiter. "Do me a favor; when you're sure we've had more than we can handle, call Steven at this number and he'll come and help you pour us into the car, okay?"

"Yes, ma'am I'll take care of you," his eyes were wide as he took the card.

"Thanks, what's your name?"

"Frank."

"Tell you what Fr…an…k. First of all don't call me ma'am again or there will be no tip. My names Jana and this is Cheryl." Both of them were laughing as the young man walked away from the table shaking his head.

"Frank, what was that all about?" the bartender asked.

"I have two cougars that are going to be drunk on their executive asses in about an hour. The one with the sexy blond highlights gave me a card to call her driver when they're done."

"Go for it. You know what they say about cougars, right?"

Reluctantly, Frank asked, "Okay, what do they say?"

"What they say is that if you want sex by ten at night you need to date a cougar as they don't have time for all the games the young females play. Hell, they have a job they need to go to early the next day and don't have time to waste."

"Take care of *your* customers; I'll take care of mine," Frank responded with ambivalence. *What is it with this guy? These women are beautiful and given the opportunity I'd take care of each of them in turn.* He smiled.

Frank placed the shrimp appetizer on the table. "Ladies, enjoy."

"Frank," Jana stated, "we didn't order this."

"I know, but I thought you could use something to eat. It's

on me." He smiled, displaying perfect teeth framed by sensuous lips. "Can I get you anything else?"

"Yes, we'd like another round," Cheryl replied.

"Are you sure?"

"Absoluuuuuuutely."

"Please bring us another around." Jana waved her finger indicating Frank should move closer, whispering in his ear, "I'll get her to eat something. Why don't you make her new drink a virgin, okay? But I want mine loaded."

"I'll take care of it." Frank smiled as he walked away. *Women no matter what age need taking care of and I'm definitely ready, willing and soooo able.* Pulling the card from his pocket he unclipped his cell phone. "May I speak to Steven? Steven, Jana is ready for you to come and pick her up. You'll need to come into the restaurant and I'll help you get them to the car. They're both rather inebriated I'm afraid."

"I'll be there in thirty minutes," Steven responded smartly.

Meeting Steven at the door, Frank escorted him to Jana's table. "Ladies, I'm here to take you home. You ready?"

"Did we call you, Steven?" Jana asked.

"Sure you did about thirty minutes ago. You asked me to come and Frank here has agreed to assist as well."

"Steven, Frank, I guess we're ready." Cheryl and Jana both stood. Steven took Cheryl's hand and wrapped his arm securely around her waist walking her to the door. Frank did the same with Jana and together they left the restaurant.

"Frank," Jana leaned over and whispered in his ear, "would you consider me forward if I gave you my phone number?"

"No. In fact if you're not busy tomorrow night could we have dinner?"

"Really, I'd loved to, but I don't know what my schedule is; call me tomorrow and we'll—*arrange*—something."

"Sure, I have your card." He waved it in front of her, "I'll give you a call."

Jana reached in her bag for a pen, grabbed back the card and wrote her personal cell number on the back. "Don't be intimidated by the card. I'm just a woman who wants to have dinner with a handsome young man."

A CEO, holy smokes, yes I can take care of her. "Not a problem, I'm fine with it. I'll call you tomorrow. Remember my name is Frank."

"Not to worry, I'll remember." She smiled as he shut the door.

Cheryl sat back and stretched out her legs as the limo moved into traffic. "I'm waiting, Jana."

"Waiting for what?"

"What question do I have to answer to be a member of your cougar club?"

"Oh, *that*," Jana sighed and turned to her friend. "It's not a simple question, the answer can be complicated. Bottom line, can you take a young man home, make love to him without *falling* in love, let him leave in the morning without remorse, but continue to see him if it pleases *you*?"

"Pleases me, no love attachment? This isn't easy—is it?"

"No, it's not. Even with Mike I had issues that almost crossed the line. I cared for him and he wanted to marry me." Jana paused and stared straight ahead. "I almost caved and said yes, not because *I* wanted to be married, but because he wanted to. It was hard, and without Charlie's help I'm not sure I would have done the right thing."

Watching Jana's face, Cheryl answered softly, "I'd like to try it, regardless of the possible shortfalls. I'm confident I can draw the line between love and sex." She laid her head back against the seat, "With all the young men in this world the possibilities are endless." She turned to look at Jana, "And I'd like a piece of that action."

"Well then, welcome to the cougar club; your benefits are limited only by your imagination."

Nine

Liza approached her mother's desk, worried about the way Jana looked. Tired was the only way to describe her. "Mom, are you okay?"

Startled, Jana looked up, "Sorry honey didn't hear you come in. I thought I was going to meet you at your dad's condo. What are you doing here?"

"We need to talk, and I didn't think we should do it in front of dad."

"Why not, he needs to be involved."

"Mom, dad's gotten much worse. He gets weaker every day. I called the doctor this morning and he said I needed to prepare myself. He said dad could go sooner than a month, the month was a guess."

"Damn! I need to go see him."

"Okay mom, but prepare yourself."

Jana's mind raced through the memories she'd had with Craig. She didn't know what to expect when she entered the condo but the man in front of her was not what she was prepared for. Craig had lost weight, he had dark circles under his eyes and his cheeks were sunken. Though he smiled when she entered the room, Jana could see the pain in his eyes. "Morning, Craig, how are you doing?"

"You're going to have to ask my nurse," he pointed toward Liza. "She's been doing a good job of taking care of me." He tried to stand and when he couldn't he simply sank into the leather chair even more. He looked to Liza, "Help me get up, please."

Jana knew how much Craig hated to ask for help from anyone. "Let me Liza, why don't you go make us some tea."

"Okay mom, all you had to do was tell me you wanted to talk to dad alone. You didn't have to send me on a useless errand."

"Liza, I need to talk to your father alone. Please make me some coffee and make it strong—thank you."

"Yes, mom."

"Jana, what's up?" Craig's voice was hoarse, strained.

"Craig, Liza called the doctor this morning because she was concerned that you're getting weaker each day. He said the month was a guess and that he really didn't know how much time you have."

"That's true, he told me that when I left the hospital yesterday. The vitamins and intravenous feeding they did, it built me up, but it was short lived. I'm not eating enough to keep a bird alive. I know this, and yet I can't eat, it just makes me sick. I can't move on my own anymore, as you've already seen, and I hurt everywhere."

She took his hand, noting it seemed smaller-colder. "What do you want me to do?"

"I've gotten all my legal papers in order, getting the stuff done for Liza helped. My will is current, my company goes to Liza." He watched Jana for her reaction, "That doesn't surprise you, does it?"

"No, that's exactly what should happen. I'm confident Liza can manage it. I think with everything else going on, she'll need the company to pull her through all this. It'll give her something to concentrate on."

"Jana, I want to say one last time how sorry I am for everything."

"Craig, there is no need to apologize for anything. We're friends and we'll always be friends."

"I know but I threw away our marriage, and for that I'm truly sorry."

"Craig stop it, we've got more important things to worry about.'

"Like what?"

"Well, and I know you're going to love and hate this when I tell you."

"Jana, give."

"Liza and Jake are expecting a baby. She had a sonogram done before she came here and it's a boy."

"Fuck Jana, I won't ever see my grandson."

"That's true, but I wanted you to know that Jake and Liza have agreed to name the baby after you, he'll be Joshua Craig. What do you think? Do you like the name?"

"Yes, I love it. You know what, it's probably right. The lord gives one life and takes another; the grand plan." Tears streaked down his cheeks as he watched Liza enter the room with coffee for her mom. "Liza, you should have told me. It's great you and Jake are expecting a baby boy. I'm so excited for you."

"Dad, I didn't tell you because it seemed so unfair to be so happy."

"Sweetheart, I'm so happy for you." He held out his arms and Liza leaned over giving him a hug and a kiss on the cheek.

"Thanks dad, we are truly blessed."

"Ladies, if one of you will help me, I'd like to go lay down for a while."

Liza took one arm and Jana the other. They helped Craig to his room and covered him with a throw. He snuggled down and was soon asleep.

"He's lost more weight than I realized," Jana said as they walked back down the hall.

"He's not eating either; it won't be long, will it mom?"

Jana hugged her daughter, trying to comfort her, "No, it won't be long. I truly believe your dad will go when he's ready."

"Mom, I think he's ready. The news of the baby was the first time I've seen him truly smile since he came home from the doctor with the news."

"You could be right, and unfortunately, though we say we prepare for this, just because we know it's going to happen doesn't make it any easier to deal with. I'm here for you sweetheart, don't forget that."

"I know mom, let's go out on the patio."

Jana stopped in the living room and picked up her coffee. It was still warm and she needed something to hold on to right now. She knew her life was about to change forever.

*****

Craig never woke up. He'd chosen his time to go and though he didn't wait a full month, he left with great happiness in his heart. Jake arrived and Liza was much calmer with him around; he settled her down. The funeral was nice, if you could say that about such a somber event. Jana closed her office for the day and Liza closed her's as well. Many people took the opportunity to pay their respects. In fact, Liza said if she received one more casserole the freezer would be full. Liza figured she wouldn't have to cook for the next year. *Why do people always bring food to the bereaved—strange habit when what the family really needed was the normalcy of cooking a meal?*

*****

Cheryl joined her again for dinner. It was a sober event and once again they were drinking their dinner. "I'm sorry; I'm not good company tonight."

"It's okay; I think we both need this. Want another drink?"

"Yes!" Jana waved her hand and Frank appeared. "We'd like another round and keep them coming."

"Can I bring you an appetizer?" Frank questioned.

"No, we've had this conversation once before, and the answer is still the same."

"I'll bring your drinks right out." Frank reached in his back pocket for the business card she'd given him before. Once again he dialed Steven.

"Steven, this is Frank again, please come pick up your boss."

"I'm outside, I'll be right in."

"Thanks, Steven."

Jana looked up as Steven walked in. "Did I call you?"

"Yes ma'am. Let me help you two to the car. Frank can you give me a hand."

"Sure," Frank whispered to Steven, "is this something they do often?"

"No, actually it's not. Jana recently buried her ex-husband and I know in spite of them not being married any more he was still one of her best friends. You take Jana and I'll help Cheryl."

"Gentlemen," Jana brushed a stray lock of hair from her face, "quit talking about us like we aren't here."

Frank put his arm around Jana's waist and helped her to her car.

She leaned over, "You didn't call me back."

"Actually I did, but you weren't in the office. They said you were out on a family emergency."

"That's true."

Frank watched tears fill her eyes. He leaned in close and kissed her softly. "It'll be fine. I'll call you tomorrow."

Ten

The office was quiet as Jana and Cheryl walked through the door. Cheryl leaned against the wall as Jana unlocked the door to her office. "God, I feel like I got hit by a truck. What was I thinking?"

"I can tell you what we weren't thinking, and that was coming to this office today. I have the worst headache I've had in years. Going out with you is bad for my health."

"Going out with me, hell this whole mess is your fault." Cheryl squinted as Jana opened the blinds to her office. "Did you hit on our waiter?"

"No, I didn't hit on our waiter." Jana relaxed in her chair, "What kind of person do you take me for?"

"I take you for a horny old woman, now come clean. You *did* hit on that young man. He was gorgeous if memory serves me right."

"Actually I didn't hit on him but I think we have a date tonight." Jana laughed in spite of the ache in her head.

"I'm going to my office and cancel all my meetings for this morning. If you need me please buzz—softly." Cheryl laughed as she walked down the hall. She'd moved to the corner office vacated by Daryl's firing. In the week Jana had been gone she'd had the room painted and new furniture put it. It was soft and elegant, similar but not the same as Jana's. She'd brought some of the furnishings from her old office, like that comfortable sofa she could lay down on with a cold cloth over her eyes. *God what a night, I haven't done that since I was in college.*

Charlied knocked on the door of Jana's office and entered slowly. When he entered he saw her sitting behind her desk going through her in-basket. *Dosen't look like a hangover to me.* "How are you doing this morning?"

"Fine, how about yourself?"

"I'm fine; would you like me to go to Starbucks and get you a latte?"

"That'd be great, but regular coffee is fine. Especially if it's ready; is it?"

"You bet, I'll get you a cup."

"Charlie, use that cup that's the size of an ocean liner, please."

Ocean liner, the lady is hungover. Smiling, Charlie left to fetch her mega cup of coffee. As he approached his desk the phone rang, "Jana Gates office, may I help you?"

"Yes, may I speak with Ms. Jana?" a soft, but baritone voice questioned.

"May I tell her who's calling?"

"Yes, tell her it's...Frank."

"Please hold on and I'll see if she's available." He buzzed Jana, "There's a young man named Frank on the phone, are you in?"

"Absolutely, thanks." She pushed the blinking light numbered 'one', "Frank, I'm glad you called. What can I do for you?"

"I'm trying to confirm our date for tonight. Are you available, or do we need to make it another night?"

"No, tonight is good what did you have in mind?"

"How about drinks and dinner at Cena's?"

"Cena's?"

"The Brazilian/Mediterranean steak house. They have great cheese bread and the food is excellent, I think you'll like it. What do you say?"

"I'm game. Do you want me to meet you there?"

"That depends."

"On what?"

"Uh—my brother showed up this morning unannounced. I hate to leave him home alone. Do you...think your friend would like to join us?"

"You mean the lady who was with me last night?"

"Yes, do you think she'd like to join us?"

"I can't speak for her, but I'll ask. Is there a number I can reach you at?"

"How about I call you back early this afternoon?"

"That works, and Frank..."

"Yes Jana."

"Thanks for calling," Jana hung up the phone and raised her hand in triumph. *Yes, he's mine.*

Charlied knocked on the door. "Who was that?"

"None of your business; have you seen Cheryl?"

"Actually no, do you want me to get her for you?"

"Yes, but I recommend you tread lightly she's not feeling well."

Charlie walked to Cheryl's office and knocked softly on her door.

"Yes, come in."

"Cheryl, Jana would like to see you if you have a minute."

"Sure, do you know if I need to bring anything?"

"No, just your smiling self. Hey, are you okay? If it's any consolation Jana looks just like you. Is this the new look for the firm's top management?"

"Not funny. We're both hurting. To tell the truth I spent the night at Jana's, but I'm not sure how we got there. It was a rough night. Don't look at me like that; it was just a couple of drinks."

"A couple and you look like this?"

"Charlie, please remember, I'm one of your bosses and you are to respect me."

"One question first?"

"Okay I'll give you one question but only one, what?"

"Do you know what a cougar is?"

"Sure, it's an elegant older woman who leads young men down the primrose path to seduction and debauchery," she smiled at the thought.

"Okay, you have my undying respect, but Jana still wants to see you."

Laughing Cheryl left her office, "Follow me young man," she said as she hooked her finger in the come hither jester.

"You two are a trip," he laughed.

Cheryl entered Jana's office, "You know your executive assistant is a smart ass. So, what's up mentor?"

"Yes I know, but you have to love him, he's good at his job," she paused, "and relatively well-trained. Now, speaking as your mentor I want you to double date with me tonight, with Frank and his brother."

"Okay," Cheryl cocked her head and narrowed her eyes, "who's Frank? Do I know him, or his brother?"

"Actually you met him last night. He was our waiter, you remember him, don't you? Cute—young—waiter?"

"Y-e-s-s, and he has a brother? You want me to go out with someone young enough to be my son?"

"Actually I don't know how old Frank's brother is. All I know is he came into town unexpectedly and Frank doesn't want to go out and leave him home alone. He asked if you'd like to join us as his brother's date. Are you game?"

"Hell, if he asked I guess I'm game. Where are we going?"

"We're having drinks and dinner at Cena."

“Nice,” Cheryl nodded, “just not sure I can drink again tonight, or tomorrow. I’m just beginning to feel somewhat normal.”

“Cheryl, one drink that’s all you have to have, and you don’t even have to finish it. Come on it’ll be fun.”

“Yes, I’ll go. Mmm, a cougar in action.”

“Do you *know* what a cougar is?”

“Sure, don’t you?”

“I do now, but I didn’t. Charlie enlightened me.”

“Really, Charlie? That explains why he asked me if I knew what a cougar was.”

“Charlie asked you that.”

“Yes, and after I told him I did he seemed very happy.”

“I think he wants a stable of cougars so he can pimp us out,” Jana laughed so hard she got the hiccups. “So...you want to join our corporate stable?”

“Definitely! Let me know when I need to be ready. I’ve got a change of clothes in my office.”

“Frank’s supposed to call me back this afternoon and when he does I’ll set it all up. We can go to dinner around seven. We should both be home in our separate beds by ten-and with any luck we won’t be alone.”

“You *are* kidding right; we can’t go to bed with these guys on the first date.”

“Tell you what, I’ll have Steven drive us tonight and if we decide we are going to get lucky, Steven can take you and Frank’s brother home and I’ll get Frank to take me home. How does that sound?”

“You’re beginning to remind me of my kid brother. He used to set up a game plan for every date with the assumption he’d get lucky. I can’t believe we’ve grown up and become like every man we’ve ever met. Have we come to this?” Cheryl relaxed and smiled, “Well, if the truth be known, I don’t have a problem with this at all. In fact it’s good on several levels. Let me know and I’ll be ready.”

"I'll give you a call as soon as I have the details. Cheryl, are you sure you're fine with all this."

"Oh, I'm more than fine. I'm ready, willing and able, really I am. Call me, I'll be waiting by my phone."

*****

Where's Charlie? The phone is ringing off the hook. "Jana Gates, may I help you?"

Frank laughed, "It's really bad when the CEO has to answer her own phone. How's your day going?"

"Frank, glad it's you, I'd hate for any of my competitors to know I had to answer my own phone. As for my day, after a half bottle of aspirin I'm beginning to feel like a human again."

"Did your friend agree to join us for dinner tonight?"

"Yes, she did; by the way her name is Cheryl."

"That's great. My brother's name is Thomas. He's very excited too. Do you want us to pick you up and if so where?"

"Tell you what. We'll both be leaving from the office so I'll have my driver take us to the restaurant. Is seven okay?"

"That's perfect. I'll make the reservations. Jana?"

"Yes, Frank."

"I'm looking forward to tonight."

"Me too, see you then."

END

Watch for the next

Cougar Tale

From

J.A. Rawls

About the Author

J.A. Rawls writes erotic romance, usually from the view of the Cougar in pursuit. She enjoys including bits of real-life travels that add to the reality and can be identified if you frequent certain cities. Reading, ballroom dancing, traveling and quilting are some of her favorite pursuits when she's not writing. J.A. is currently working on several other erotic romances to include her sexy 'Cougar' series, stories of older women and their younger men.

Enjoy These Other Romance Divine Selections by J.A. Rawls

3-Way Weekend

ISBN: 978-1-934446-23-2

It's supposed to be a 'girls-get-away-weekend' but weather problems leave Jana left alone in a Denver hotel. What's a girl to do but make the best of the situation? Fortunately, identical twins Tim and Tom come to her rescue, and Jana learns about the stamina of youth and her own capacities as a woman.

Play It Again Sam

ISBN: 978-1-934446-33-1

Susan Masters worked her way out of a bad marriage and up the company ladder. But now she was stalled, both at the company, and with trying to juggle two men in her life. Can she really handle a third man, or is this the one was she meant for? A sexy interlude in a cabana takes her to a new level of sensuous exploration, but leaves her with a little problem. Can a woman really have it all?

Nation's Call

ISBN: 978-1-934446-38-6

Technical Sergeant Tom Weston was returning to the combat zone, and this time he had TSgt Amy Adams and TSgt Melissa Mathews as part of his team. Could they survive what they'd encounter: the danger of a fire fight on the street, the needs of two women and one man? It's life and death, lust and love when they answer *Nation's Call*.

Man-Oh-Man

ISBN: 978-1-934446-19-5

Gary was at a loss; a meaningful relationship eluded him. He wasn't sure what - or who - he wanted. Could two strangers he met on a plane provide the answer? One erotic night with new friends Jim and Martin shows Gary what is possible.

Angel's Delight

ISBN: 978-1-934446-28-7

In a new town, at a new job, Angel Jamison was waiting for Mister Right, but if he didn't come soon, she might settle for Mr. 'Right Now.' Could one of her bosses, Scott or Steve, be 'Mr. Right?' Or could it be both of them? A wild night in the desert allows this cactus flower to come to full bloom. And the consequences…?

All I Want for Christmas

ISBN: 978-1-934446-31-7

All I Want for Christmas is the sequel to author J.A. Rawls sexy threesome *Angel's Delight*. Angel's friend Janice is down on her luck and desperately needs both a job – and a man. Can Santa deliver? Sparks fly when Steve goes to Denver to move Janice to Tucson; it's a trip in which tempers and passions flare. In Tucson, Angel, Janice, Scott and Steve are together again, but how close will the relationship get, and can Angel make good on the pact she broke with Janice?

Christmas Creep

ISBN: 978-1-934446-60-7

Liz dreaded the oncoming holiday season, which seemed to arrive earlier every year. It was hard to get and stay in the spirit for months-so why do it at all? Could a winter storm and two stranded snow plow drivers help her overcome the *Christmas Creep?*

BJ's Cowboys

ISBN: 978-1-934446-75-1

When BJ stops by her old home town she's not sure what she's searching for, or what she'll find. Was she looking to put the past behind her—or resurrect it? Her old lover, Bill, has his own ideas, of what he let get away, and what he wants now. It only takes a weekend with old *friends* Bill and Herman for her to put her claim on *BJ's Cowboys*.

Elf at Play

ISBN: 978-1-934446-97-3

Evelyn Louise Freeman, Elf to her friends, was at a crossroads. Her parents were recently deceased and Elf had fulfilled neither of their desires. Her mother had wanted her to find a husband and her father envisioned her as a career woman. With the holidays approaching, Elf journeys to Washington DC, hoping that a new environment will be what she needs to make it all right. A dashing Frenchman turns her life around and the holiday takes on a new meaning when there is an Elf at Play.

Also Available From Romance Divine LLC at:
www.romancedivine.cm
and
Other fine e-book and print book retailers.

From author Andrea Glenn

Safe Haven
Miami Desire
The Coffee Shop
Style of a Lifetime
A Dark Night in Paris

From author Bryn Colvin

Late Night Sessions (Also in print)
Rekindling the Belfire

From author Bailey Griffin

Simply Suitable

From Author Ronna Gage

Bare It All
Love Lessons
Friends and Lovers
First Thanksgiving

From author Sarah J. Head

At Home and Away
(Available as e-book, print and audio book)

From Author Wynter O'Reilly

Peppermint Kisses

From author Mary Suzanne

Addie
Secrets
Partners
Marooned
Loving Katie
Fantasy Games
Angel In Blue
My Cowboys
Darling Rebel
Sexual Knead
Spanish Rose
Private Dancer
Rekindled Love
Just Not Into Me
Chance Encounter
The Christmas Gift
A New Beginning
Double Your Pleasure
Torn Between Two Loves
And, in print:
SEXY: Mary Suzanne's Erotic Romance Collection

From Author Elizabeth Black

Feral Heat
Fountain of Youth
Indiscretions Vol. I
Tinsel Temptations

From Gregory Causey and Natasha Yushanov

Dancing With Natasha (Also in Print)

From Author Gregory Causey

Hitler's Will (Also in print)

From Author Deborah A. Hodge

The Calling (Also in print)

From Author Carol Cassada

Going Home Again

From Danny Causey and Gregory Causey

Denizens of the Desert
(Print: Photographs by Danny Causey;
Edited by Greg Causey)

From author Jodi Olson

Getting Wild
Playing House
Sinful Delights
A Christmas Wish
Storm's Obsession
Claiming Lauren
Raining on Sunday
Naughty Whispers
Breathless Whispers
Hunter's Possession
Home for Christmas
Tempting Pleasures (Print)
Sensuous Pleasure (Print)
Seduction - The Riley Way
Madame Bree and the Sheriff

www.ingramcontent.com/pod-product-compliance
Lightning Source LLC
Chambersburg PA
CBHW030339310726
48979CB00001B/98

* 9 7 8 1 9 3 4 4 4 6 9 8 0 *